nickelodeon™

SANJAY & CRAIG™

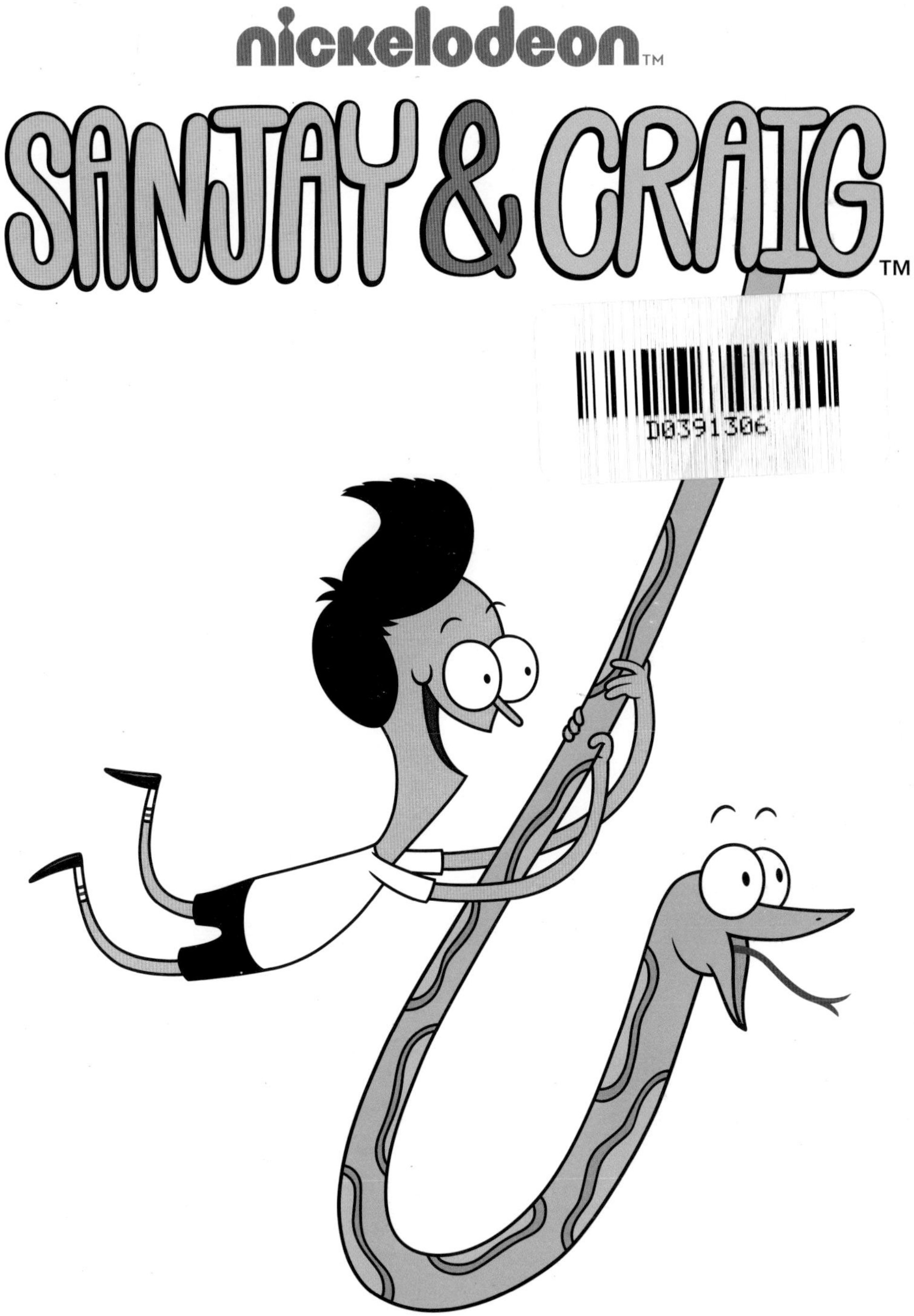

PAPERCUTZ™
New York

nickelodeon GRAPHIC NOVELS AVAILABLE FROM PAPERCUTZ

nickelodeon
SANJAY AND CRAIG
FIGHT THE FUTURE WITH FLAVOR!
PAPERCUTZ

#1 "Fight the Future with Flavor"

nickelodeon
SANJAY AND CRAIG
NEW KID ON THE BLOCK
PAPERCUTZ

#2 "New Kid on the Block"

nickelodeon
BREADWINNERS
JOURNEY TO THE BOTTOM OF THE SEATS
PAPERCUTZ

#1 "Journey to the Bottom of the Seats"

COMING SOON!

nickelodeon
HARVEY BEAKS
INSIDE JOKE
PAPERCUTZ

#1 "Inside Joke"

COMING SOON!

nickelodeon
PIG GOAT BANANA CRICKET
Orgle Borgle Selfie Simple-Dee-Doo!
PAPERCUTZ

#1 "Orgle Borgle Selfie Simple-Dee-Doo!"

Nickelodeon graphic novels are available for $7.99 in paperback, $12.99 in hardcover. Available from booksellers everywhere. You can also order online from Papercutz.com, or call 1-800-886-1223, Monday through Friday, 9-5 EST. MC, Visa, and AmEx accepted. To order by mail, please add $4.00 for postage and handling for first book ordered, $1.00 for each additional book and make check payable to NBM Publishing.
Send to: Papercutz, 160 Broadway, Suite 700, East Wing, New York, NY 10038.

Nickelodeon graphic novels are also available digitally wherever e-books are sold.

SUBSCRIBE!

The Greatest Kids Magazine in the world is here and you can be a charter subscriber. Be the first to get your copies and make sure you don't miss a single issue of the all-new Nickelodeon Magazine!

nickelodeon MAGAZINE
THE GREATEST KIDS MAGAZINE IN THE WORLD IS HERE!
Featuring All-New COMICS!
BOOO!
nickelodeon MAGAZINE
HARVEY BEAKS
HALLOWEEN

Never miss an issue of nickelodeon™ MAGAZINE

Get Your Copies Delivered Right to Your Mailbox at Home!

Save! And Get Free Issues!

7 ISSUES FOR THE PRICE OF 6!

+SAVE $7 OFF COVER PRICE!

6 REGULAR ISSUES
+1 BONUS FREE ISSUE
7 ISSUES FOR ONLY $27.50

14 ISSUES FOR THE PRICE OF 12!

+SAVE $14 OFF COVER PRICE!

12 REGULAR ISSUES
+2 BONUS FREE ISSUES
14 ISSUES FOR ONLY $49.99

DIGITAL SUBSCRIPTION - ONLY $19.99 - OR FREE FOR ALL PRINT SUBSCRIBERS!

ORDER ONLINE at Papercutz.com/nickmag

OR CALL 1-800-778-6278

(Please have debit/credit card ready)

Use promo code: SACGN2.

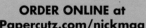

DUDE!

nickelodeon™

SANJAY AND CRAIG™

TABLE OF CONTENTS

WITHDRAWN

SANJAY AND CRAIG™

2 "NEW KID ON THE BLOCK"

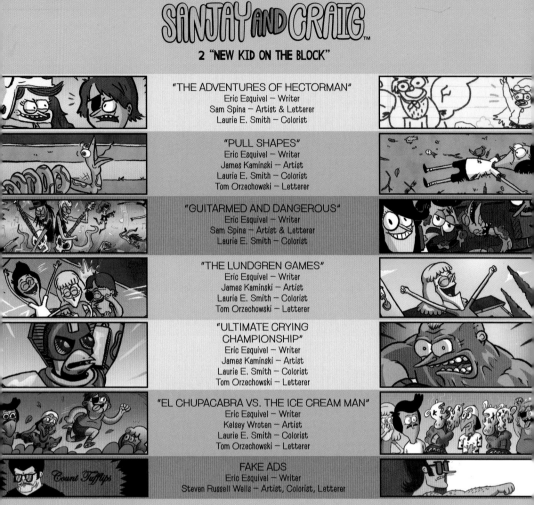

"THE ADVENTURES OF HECTORMAN"
Eric Esquivel — Writer
Sam Spina — Artist & Letterer
Laurie E. Smith — Colorist

"PULL SHAPES"
Eric Esquivel — Writer
James Kaminski — Artist
Laurie E. Smith — Colorist
Tom Orzechowski — Letterer

"GUITARMED AND DANGEROUS"
Eric Esquivel — Writer
Sam Spina — Artist & Letterer
Laurie E. Smith — Colorist

"THE LUNDGREN GAMES"
Eric Esquivel — Writer
James Kaminski — Artist
Laurie E. Smith — Colorist
Tom Orzechowski — Letterer

"ULTIMATE CRYING CHAMPIONSHIP"
Eric Esquivel — Writer
James Kaminski — Artist
Laurie E. Smith — Colorist
Tom Orzechowski — Letterer

"EL CHUPACABRA VS. THE ICE CREAM MAN"
Eric Esquivel — Writer
Kelsey Wroten — Artist
Laurie E. Smith — Colorist
Tom Orzechowski — Letterer

FAKE ADS
Eric Esquivel — Writer
Steven Russell Wells — Artist, Colorist, Letterer

Based on the Nickelodeon animated TV series created by Jim Dirschberger, Andreas Trolf, and Jay Howell.

James Salerno — Sr. Art Director/Nickelodeon
Chris Nelson — Design/Production
Jeff Whitman — Production Coordinator
Bethany Bryan — Editor
Joan Hilty — Comics Editor/Nickelodeon
Emily Wixted, Asante Simons — Editorial Interns
Jim Salicrup
Editor-in-Chief

ISBN: 978-1-62991-425-1 paperback edition
ISBN: 978-1-62991-426-8 hardcover edition

Copyright © 2016 Viacom International Inc. All rights reserved. Nickelodeon, Sanjay and Craig, Breadwinners, Harvey Beaks, Pig Goat Banana Cricket and all related titles, logos and characters are trademarks of Viacom International Inc. Any similarity to real people and places in fiction or seni fiction is purely coincidental.
Papercutz books may be purchased for business or promotional use. For information on bulk purchases please contact Macmillan Corporate and Premium Sales Department at (800) 221-7945 x5442.

Printed in China
January 2016 by Toppan Leefung Printing Limited
Jin Ju Guan Li Qu,
Da Ling Shan Town,
Dongguan, PRC
China

Distributed by Macmillan

First Printing

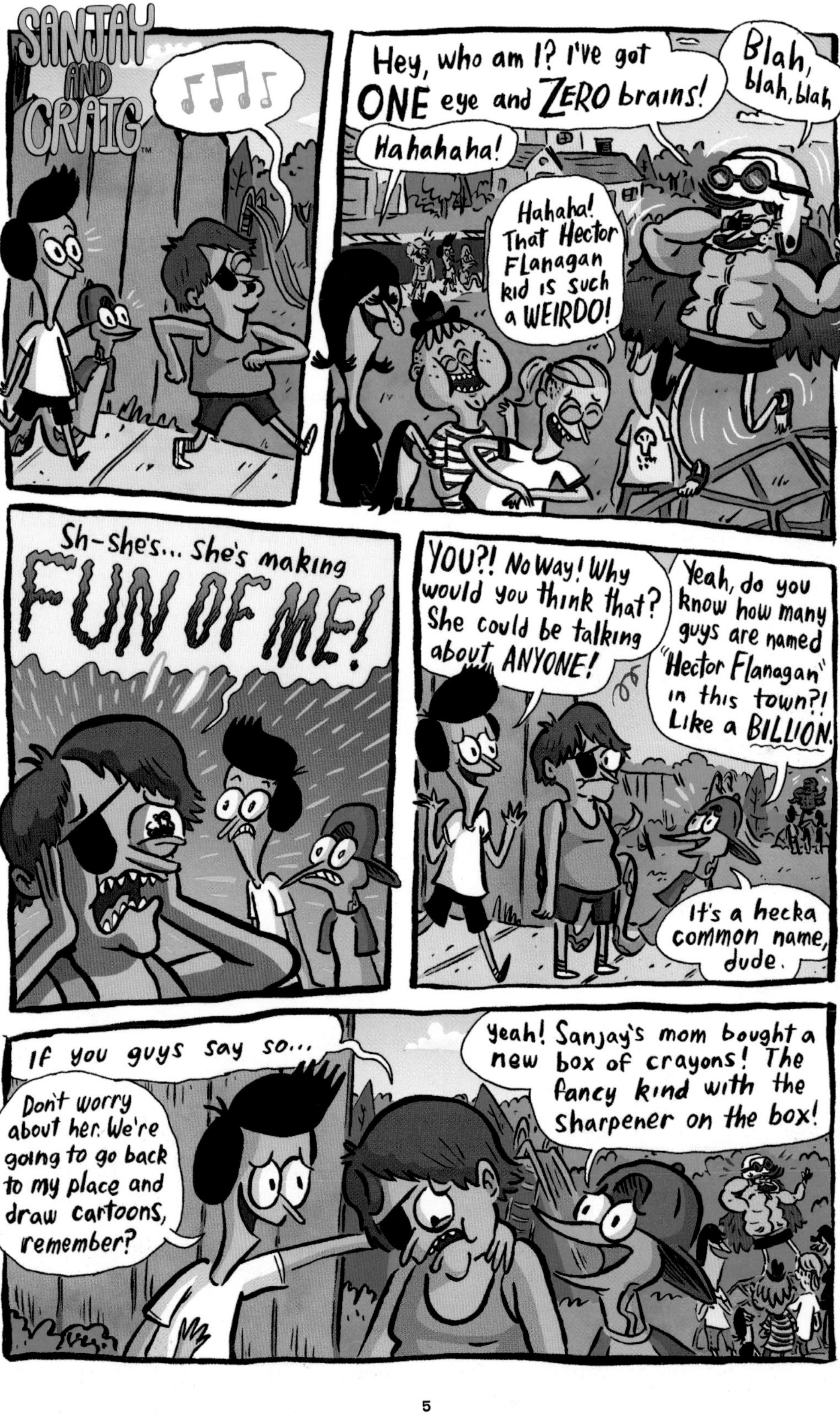
SANJAY AND CRAIG™
Hey, who am I? I've got ONE eye and ZERO brains!
Blah, blah, blah
Hahahaha!
Hahaha! That Hector Flanagan kid is such a WEIRDO!
Sh-she's... she's making FUN OF ME!
YOU?! No Way! Why would you think that? She could be talking about ANYONE!
Yeah, do you know how many guys are named "Hector Flanagan" in this town?! Like a BILLION.
It's a hecka common name, dude.
If you guys say so...
Don't worry about her. We're going to go back to my place and draw cartoons, remember?
Yeah! Sanjay's mom bought a new box of crayons! The fancy kind with the sharpener on the box!

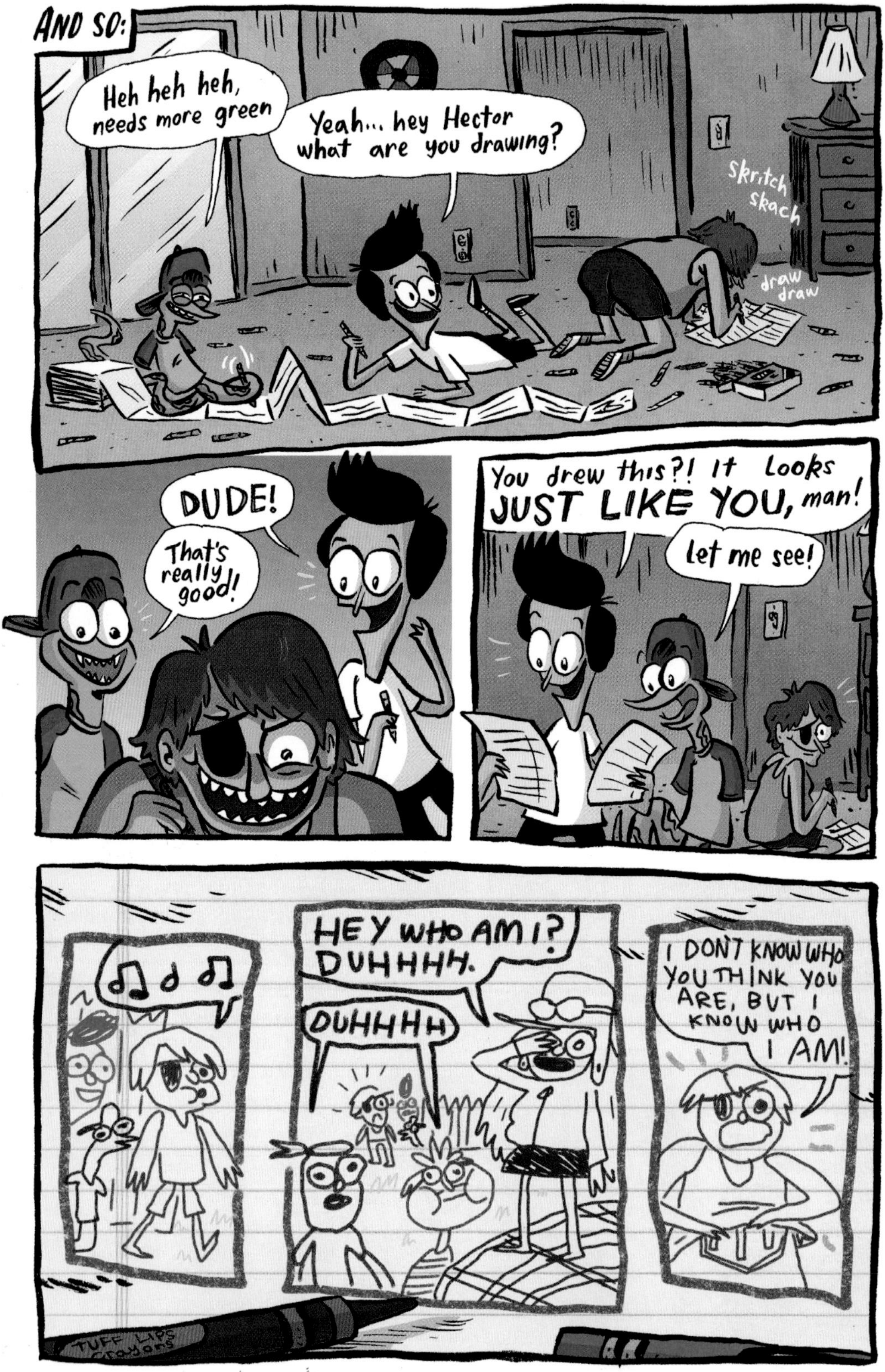
AND SO:
Heh heh heh, needs more green
Yeah... hey Hector what are you drawing?
Skritch skach
draw draw
DUDE!
That's really good!
You drew this?! It Looks JUST LIKE YOU, man!
let me see!
HEY WHO AM I? DUHHHH.
DUHHHH
I DON'T KNOW WHO YOU THINK YOU ARE, BUT I KNOW WHO I AM!
TUFF LIPS Crayons

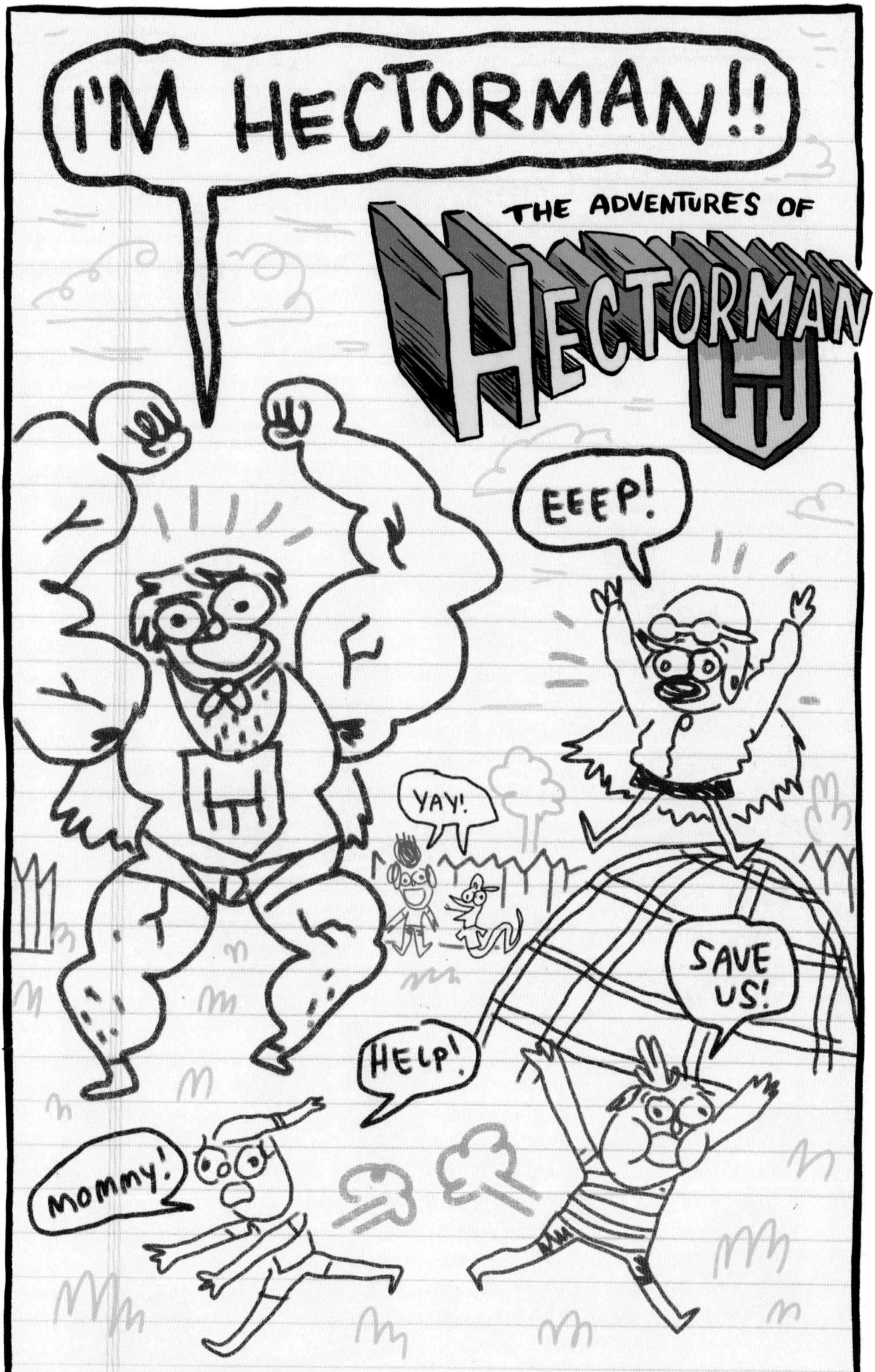
I'M HECTORMAN!!
THE ADVENTURES OF
HECTORMAN
EEEP!
YAY!
SAVE US!
HELP!
MOMMY!

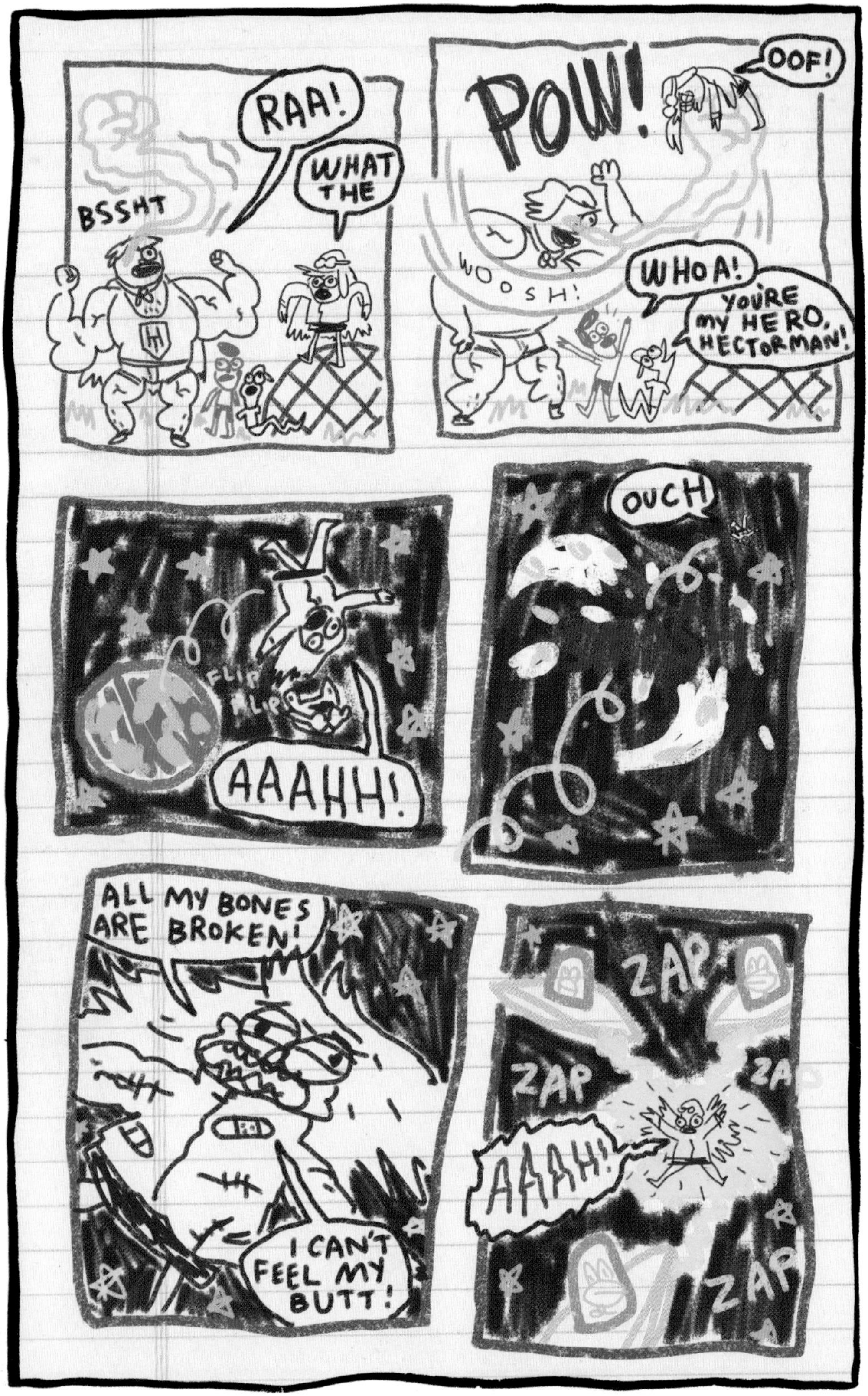
RAA!
WHAT THE
BSSHT
POW!
OOF!
WOOSH!
WHOA!
YOU'RE MY HERO, HECTORMAN!
FLIP FLIP
AAAHH!
OUCH
ALL MY BONES ARE BROKEN!
I CAN'T FEEL MY BUTT!
ZAP
ZAP
ZAP
ZAP
AAAH!

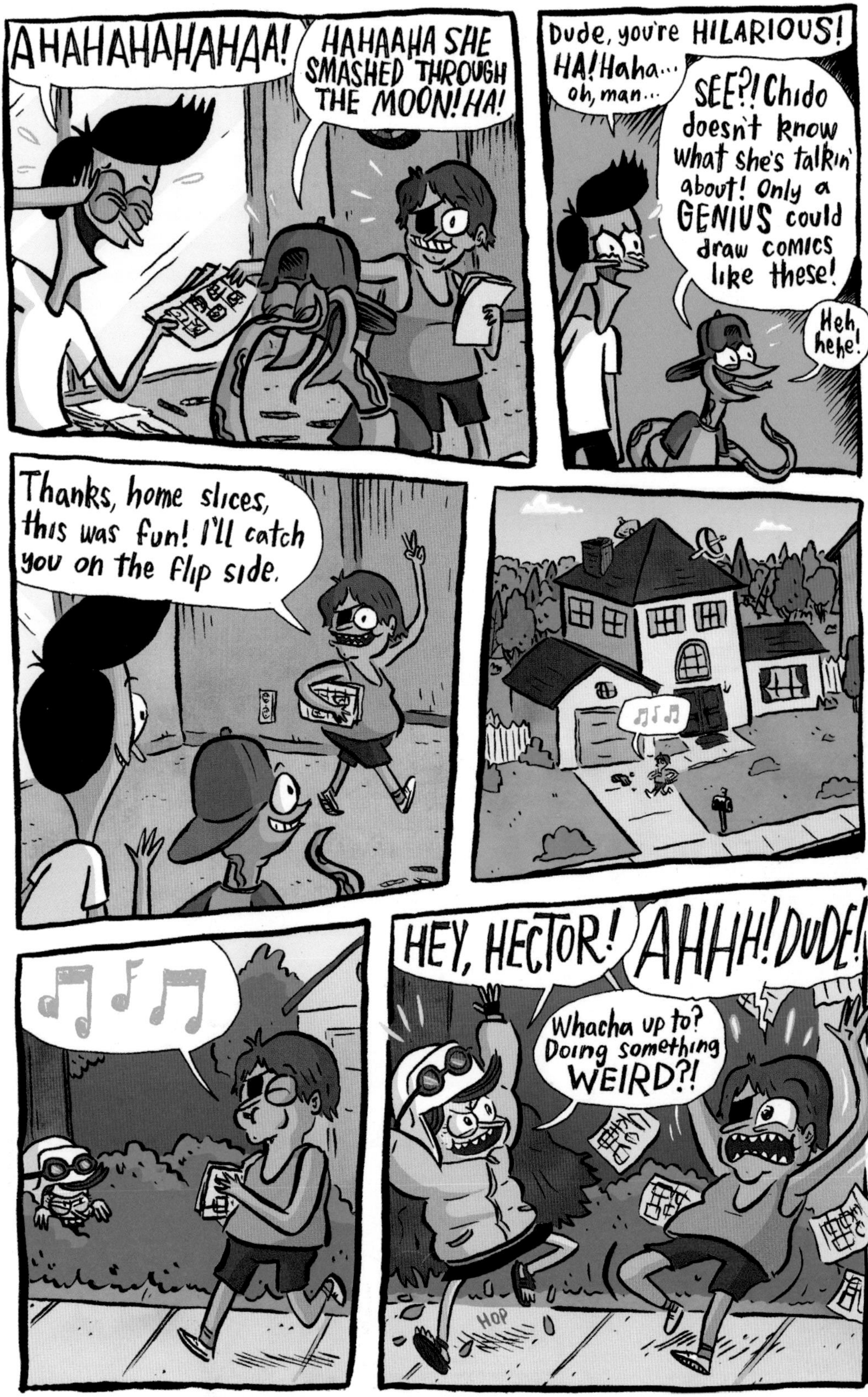
AHAHAHAHAHAA!
HAHAAHA SHE SMASHED THROUGH THE MOON! HA!
Dude, you're HILARIOUS!
HA! Haha... oh, man...
SEE?! Chido doesn't know what she's talkin' about! Only a GENIUS could draw comics like these!
Heh, hehe!
Thanks, home slices, this was fun! I'll catch you on the flip side.
HEY, HECTOR!
AHHH! DUDE!
Whacha up to? Doing something WEIRD?!
HOP

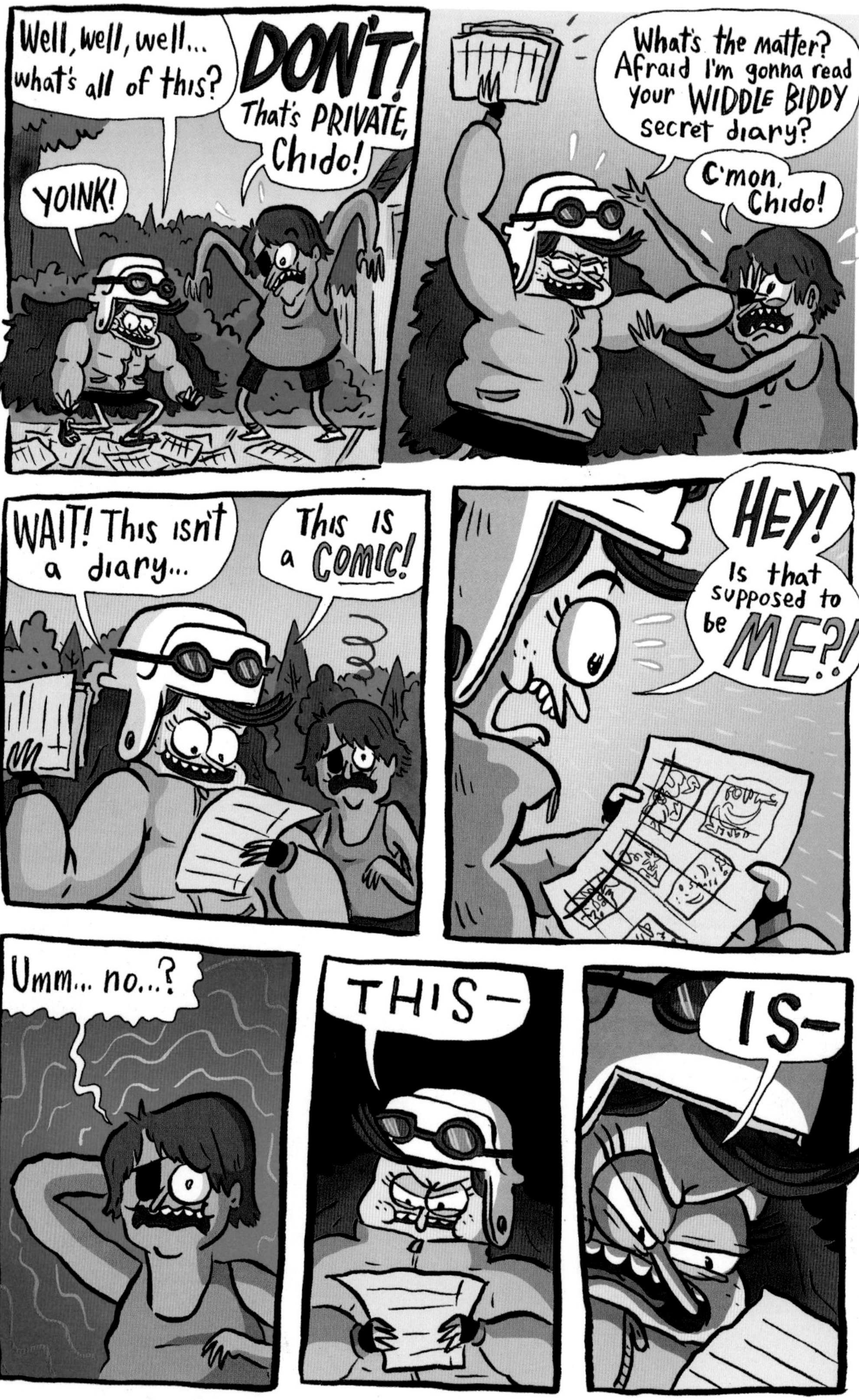
Well, well, well...
what's all of this?
YOINK!
DON'T!
That's PRIVATE,
Chido!
What's the matter?
Afraid I'm gonna read
your WIDDLE BIDDY
secret diary?
C'mon,
Chido!
WAIT! This isn't
a diary...
This is
a COMIC!
HEY!
Is that
supposed to
be ME?!
Umm... no...?
THIS—
IS—

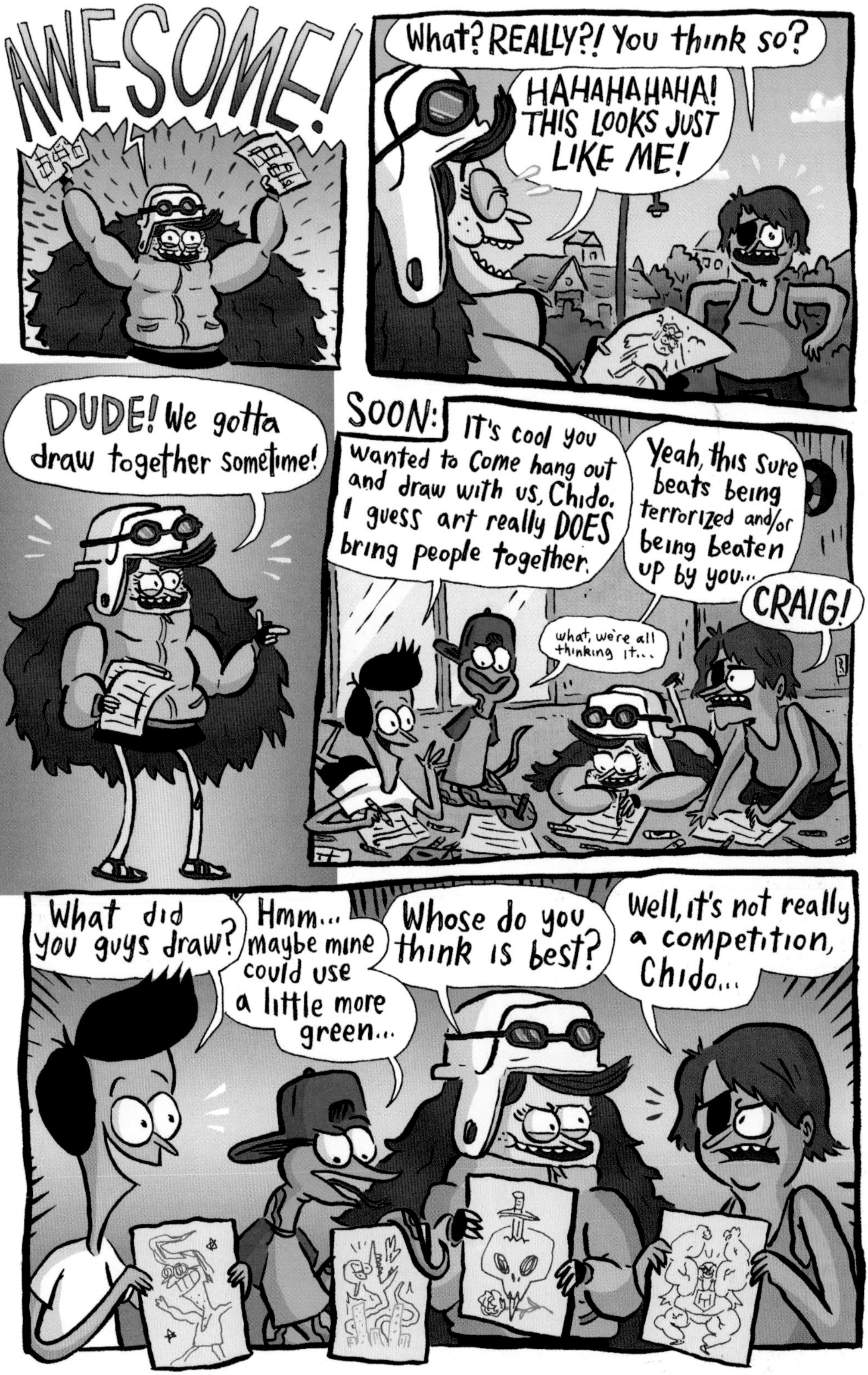
AWESOME!
What? REALLY?! You think so?
HAHAHAHAHA! THIS LOOKS JUST LIKE ME!
DUDE! We gotta draw together sometime!
SOON:
IT's cool you wanted to come hang out and draw with us, Chido. I guess art really DOES bring people together.
Yeah, this sure beats being terrorized and/or being beaten up by you...
what, we're all thinking it...
CRAIG!
What did you guys draw?
Hmm... maybe mine could use a little more green...
Whose do you think is best?
Well, it's not really a competition, Chido...

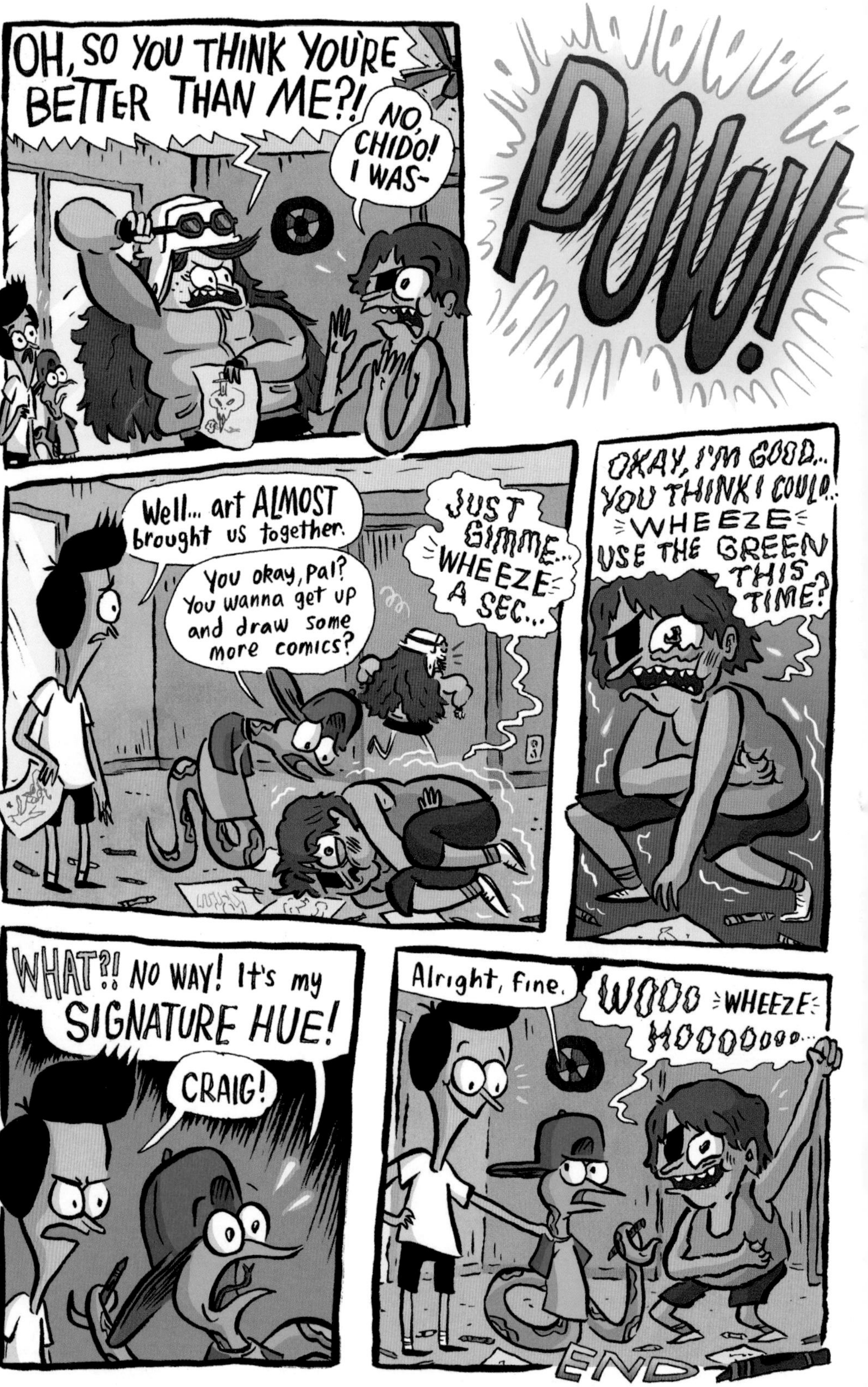
OH, SO YOU THINK YOU'RE BETTER THAN ME?!
NO, CHIDO! I WAS-
POW!
Well... art ALMOST brought us together.
You okay, pal? You wanna get up and draw some more comics?
JUST GIMME... WHEEZE A SEC...
OKAY, I'M GOOD... YOU THINK I COULD... WHEEZE USE THE GREEN THIS TIME?
WHAT?! NO WAY! It's my SIGNATURE HUE!
CRAIG!
Alright, fine.
WOOO WHEEZE HOOOOooo...
END

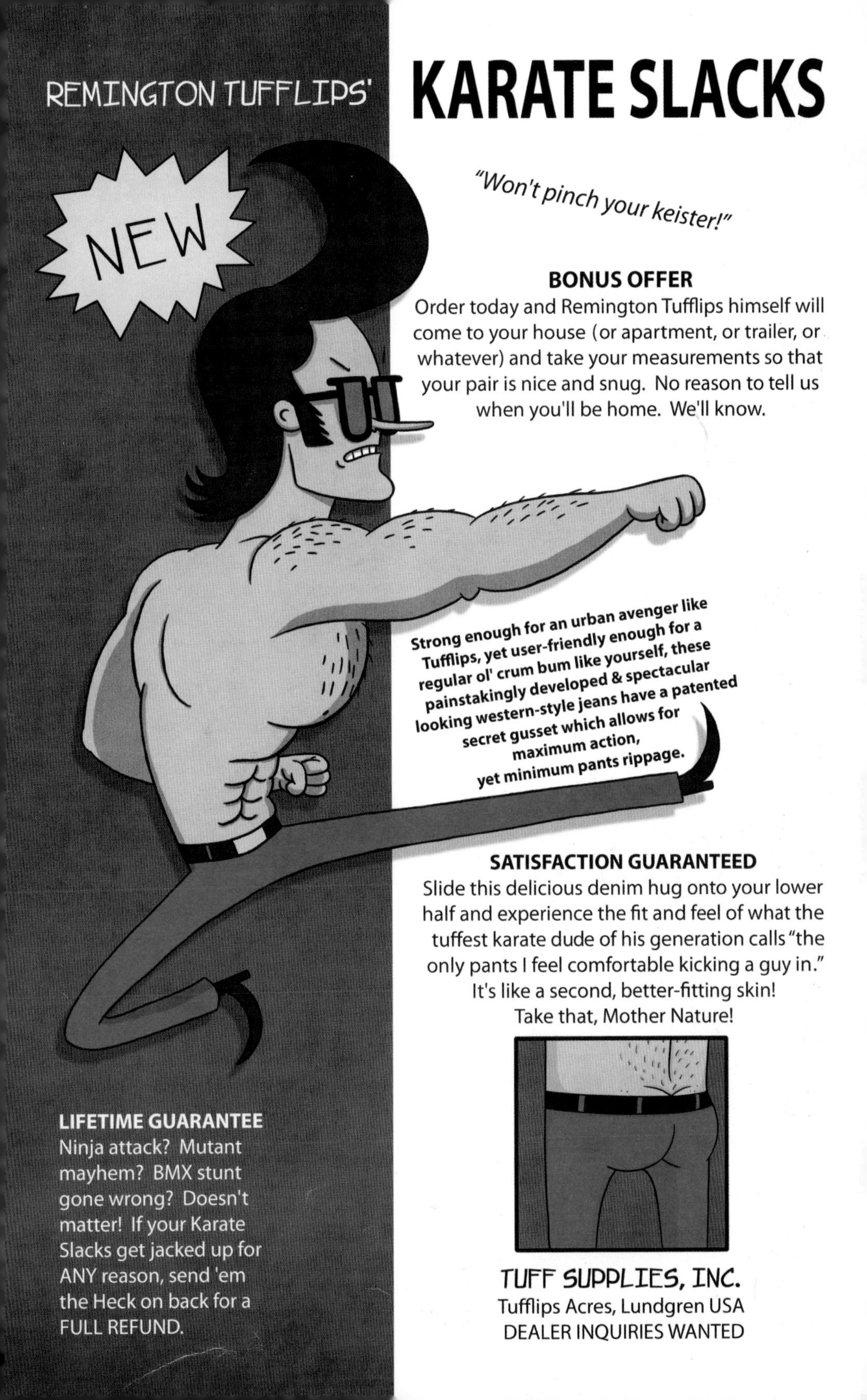
REMINGTON TUFFLIPS'
KARATE SLACKS
NEW
"Won't pinch your keister!"
BONUS OFFER
Order today and Remington Tufflips himself will come to your house (or apartment, or trailer, or whatever) and take your measurements so that your pair is nice and snug. No reason to tell us when you'll be home. We'll know.
Strong enough for an urban avenger like Tufflips, yet user-friendly enough for a regular ol' crum bum like yourself, these painstakingly developed & spectacular looking western-style jeans have a patented secret gusset which allows for maximum action, yet minimum pants rippage.
SATISFACTION GUARANTEED
Slide this delicious denim hug onto your lower half and experience the fit and feel of what the tuffest karate dude of his generation calls "the only pants I feel comfortable kicking a guy in." It's like a second, better-fitting skin! Take that, Mother Nature!
LIFETIME GUARANTEE
Ninja attack? Mutant mayhem? BMX stunt gone wrong? Doesn't matter! If your Karate Slacks get jacked up for ANY reason, send 'em the Heck on back for a FULL REFUND.
TUFF SUPPLIES, INC.
Tufflips Acres, Lundgren USA
DEALER INQUIRIES WANTED

SANJAY AND CRAIG™ in "Pull Shapes"

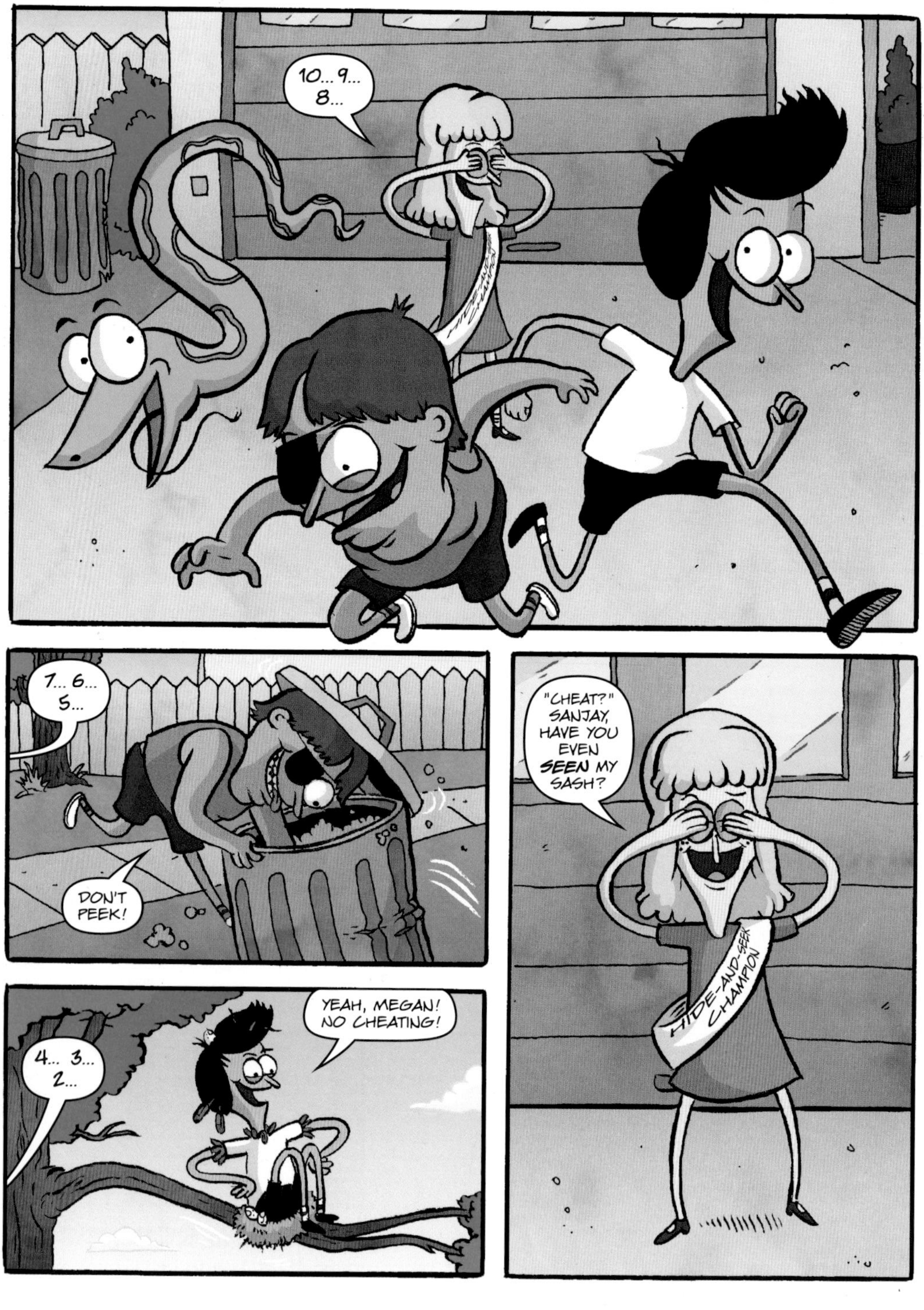
10... 9... 8...
HIDE-AND-SEEK CHAMPION
7... 6... 5...
DON'T PEEK!
4... 3... 2...
YEAH, MEGAN! NO CHEATING!
"CHEAT?" SANJAY, HAVE YOU EVEN **SEEN** MY SASH?
HIDE-AND-SEEK CHAMPION

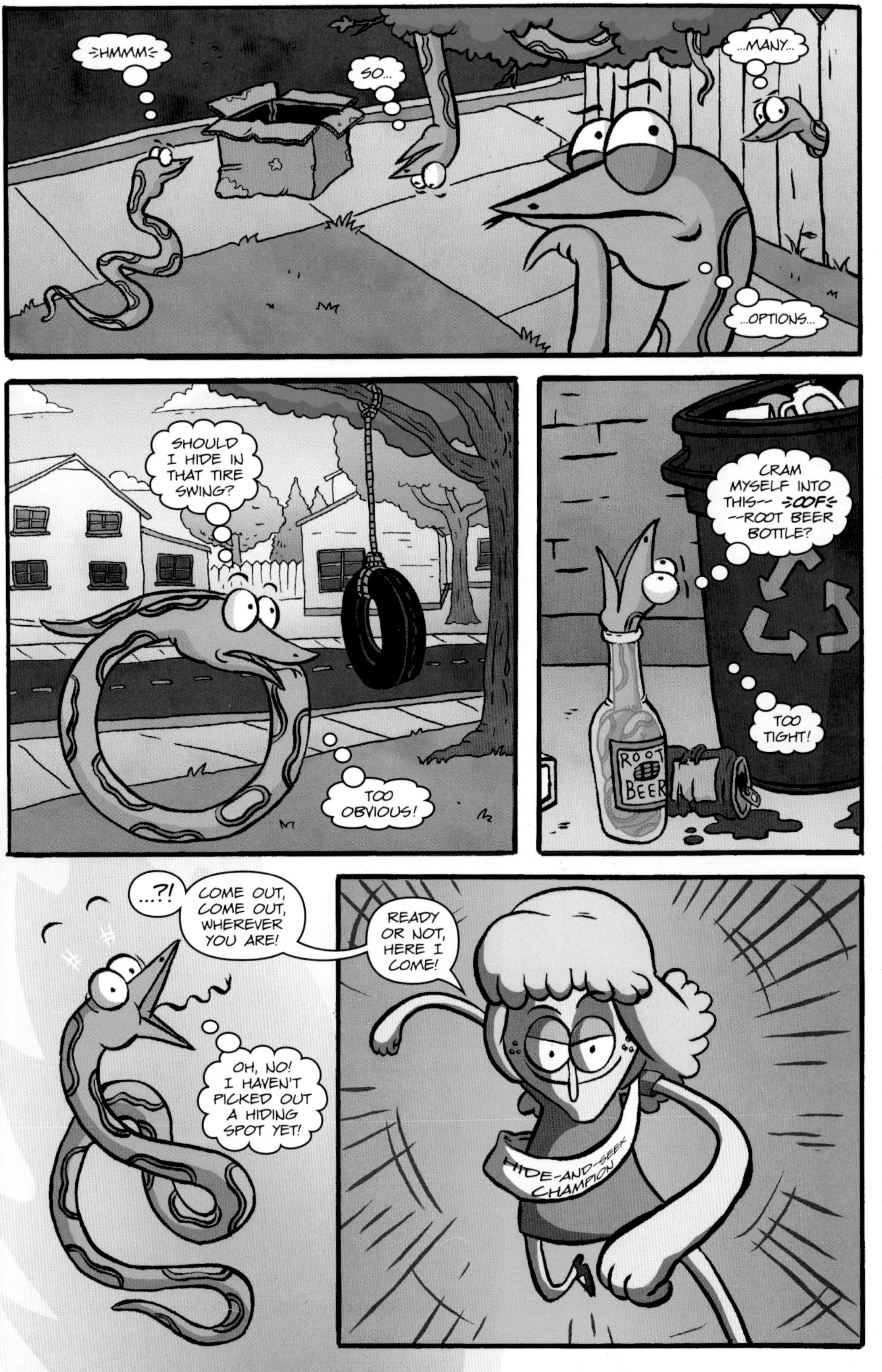
HMMM
SO...
...MANY...
...OPTIONS...
SHOULD I HIDE IN THAT TIRE SWING?
TOO OBVIOUS!
CRAM MYSELF INTO THIS-- OOF --ROOT BEER BOTTLE?
ROOT BEER
TOO TIGHT!
...?!
COME OUT, COME OUT, WHEREVER YOU ARE!
READY OR NOT, HERE I COME!
OH, NO! I HAVEN'T PICKED OUT A HIDING SPOT YET!
HIDE-AND-SEEK CHAMPION

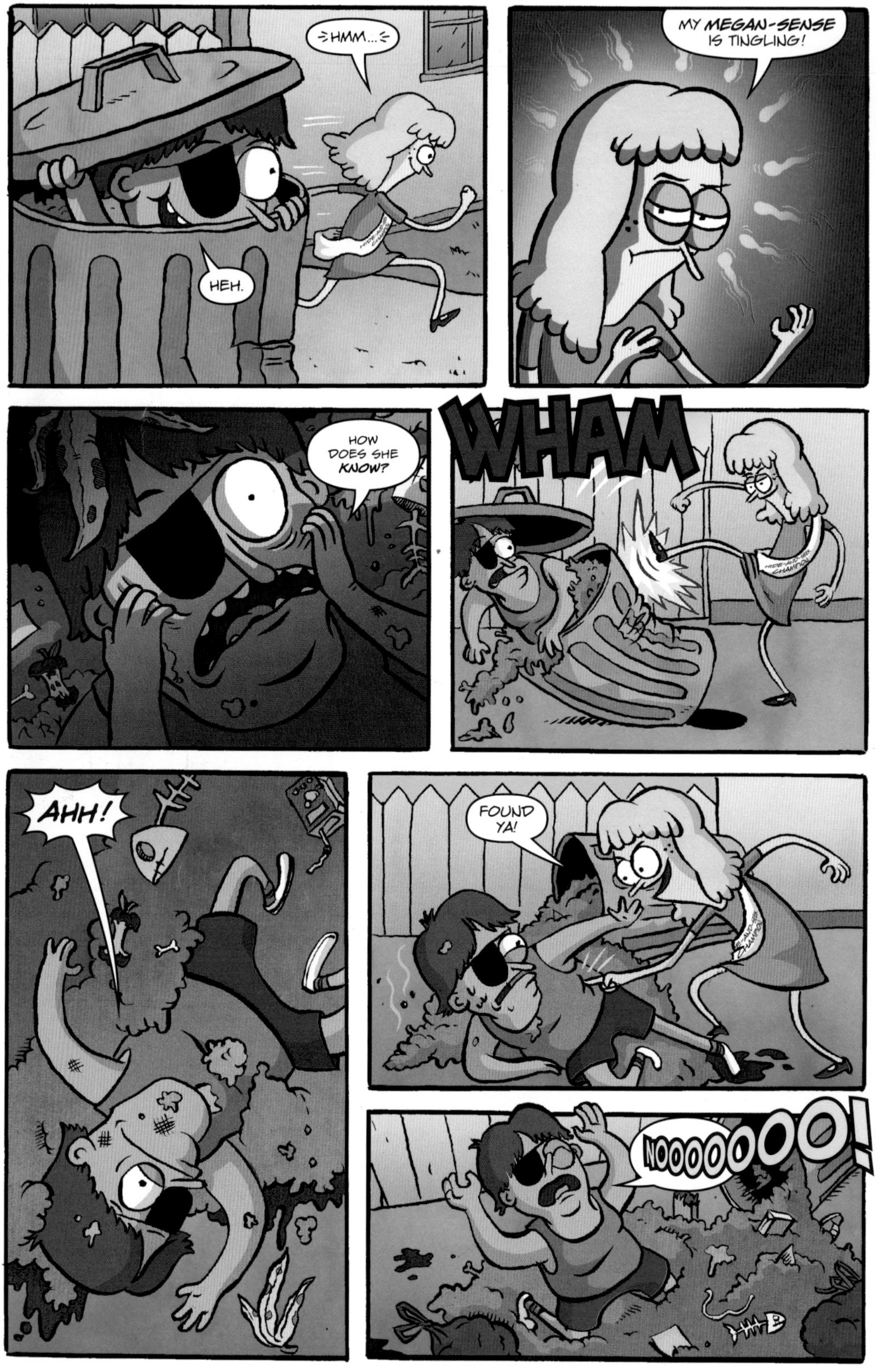
HMM...
HEH.
MY MEGAN-SENSE IS TINGLING!
HOW DOES SHE KNOW?
WHAM
AHH!
FOUND YA!
NOOOOOOOO!

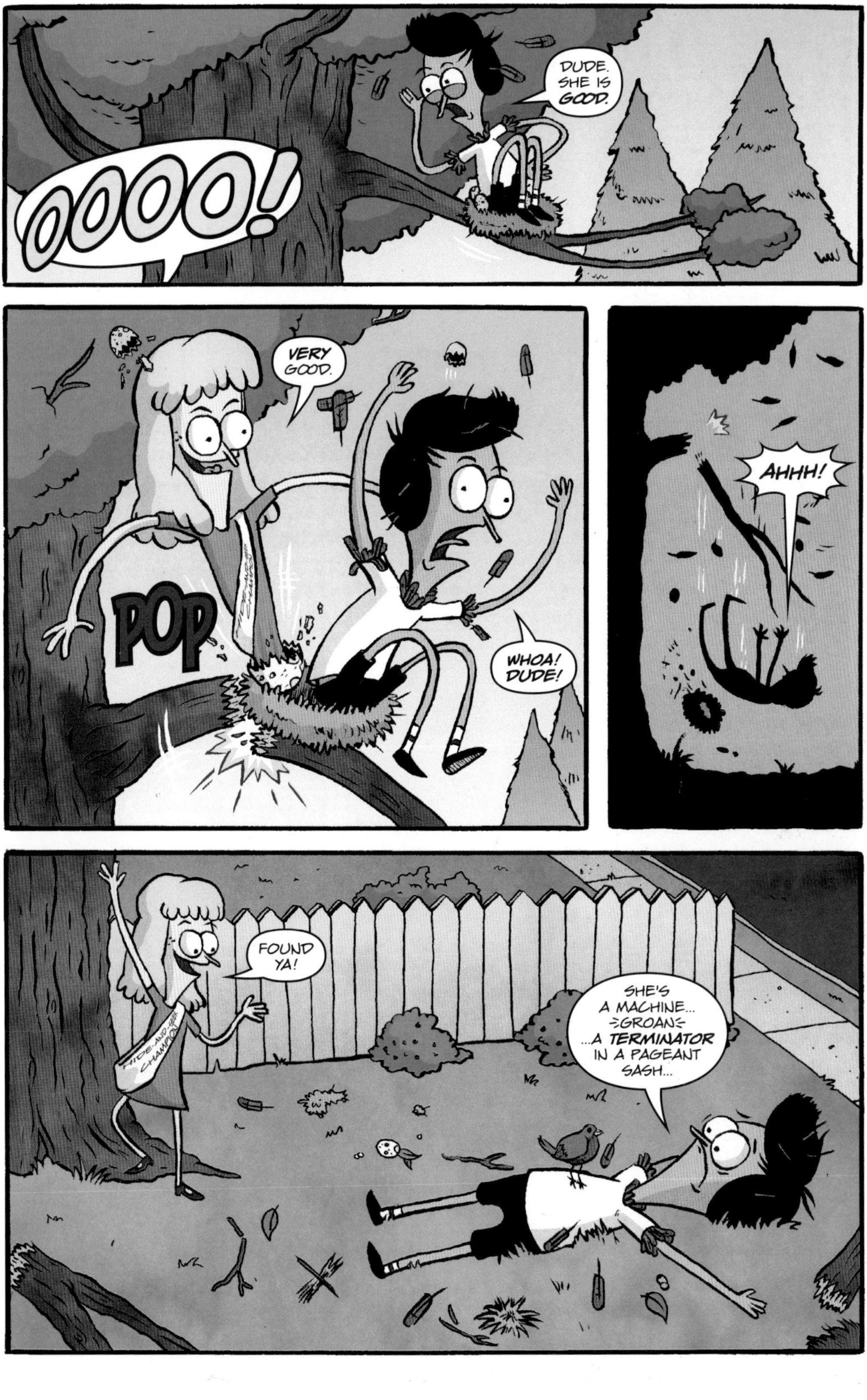
DUDE. SHE IS GOOD.
OOOO!
VERY GOOD.
POP
WHOA! DUDE!
AHHH!
FOUND YA!
SHE'S A MACHINE... GROAN ...A TERMINATOR IN A PAGEANT SASH...

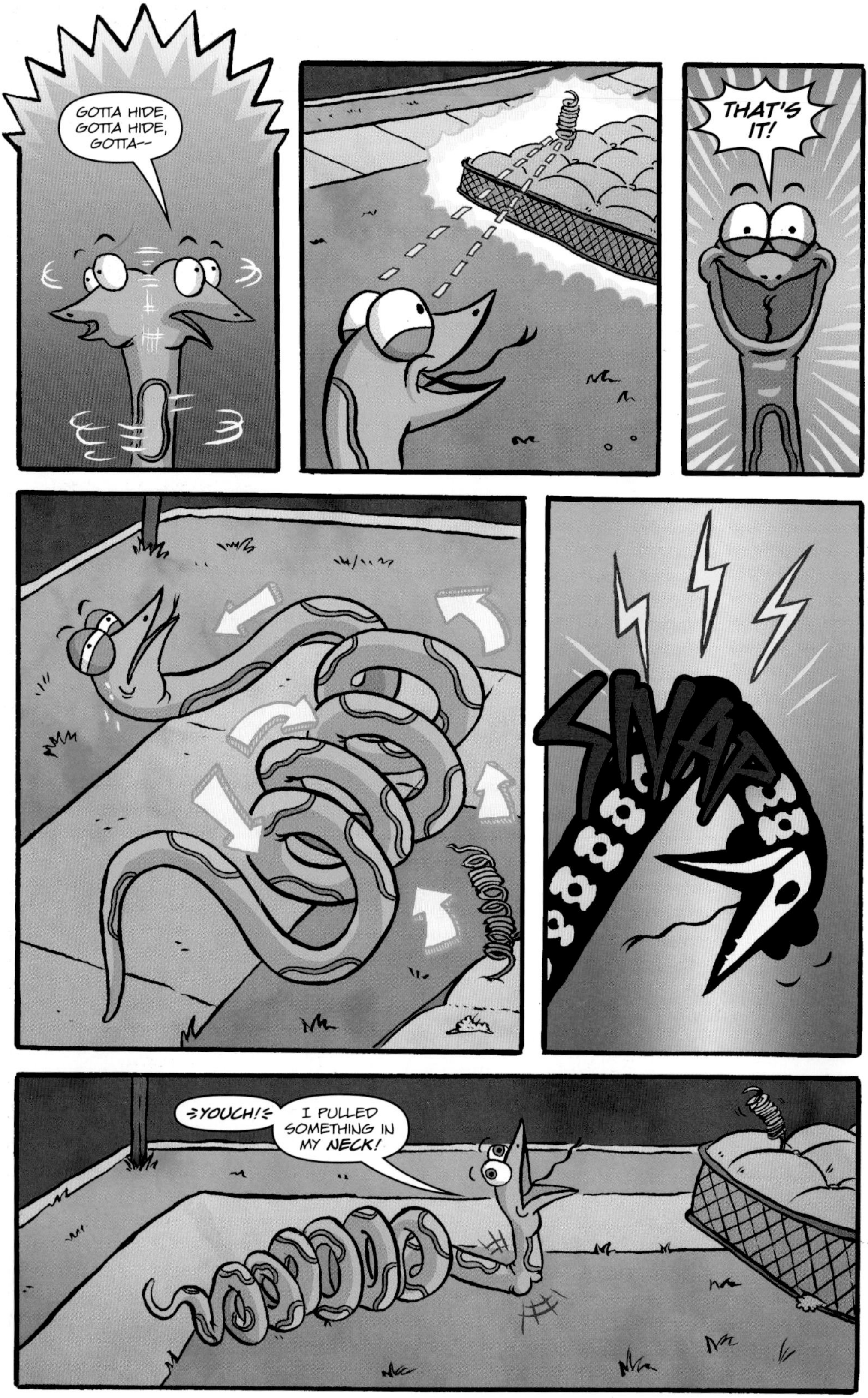

GOTTA HIDE, GOTTA HIDE, GOTTA--
THAT'S IT!
SNAP
YOUCH!
I PULLED SOMETHING IN MY NECK!

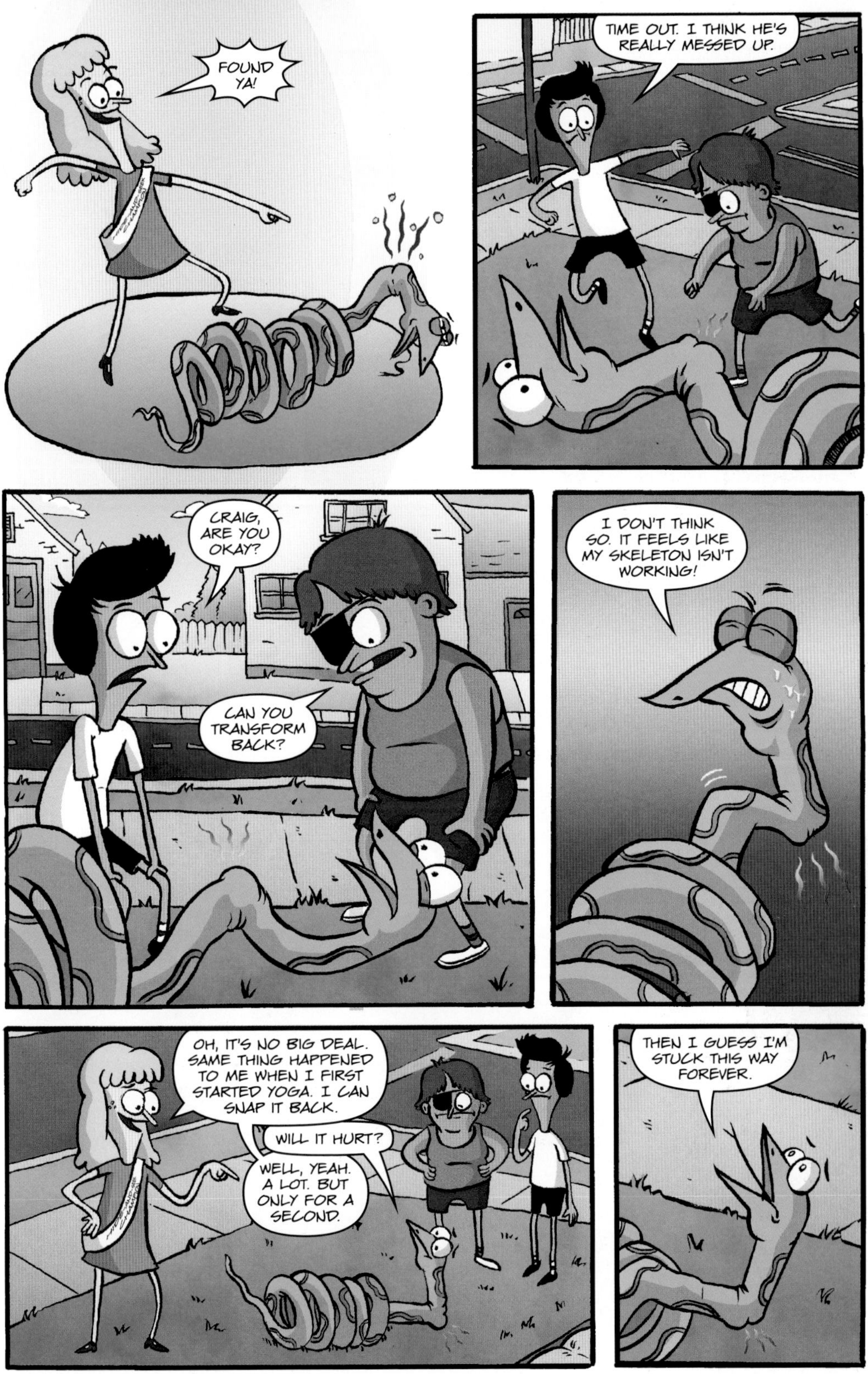
FOUND YA!
TIME OUT. I THINK HE'S REALLY MESSED UP.
CRAIG, ARE YOU OKAY?
CAN YOU TRANSFORM BACK?
I DON'T THINK SO. IT FEELS LIKE MY SKELETON ISN'T WORKING!
OH, IT'S NO BIG DEAL. SAME THING HAPPENED TO ME WHEN I FIRST STARTED YOGA. I CAN SNAP IT BACK.
WILL IT HURT?
WELL, YEAH. A LOT. BUT ONLY FOR A SECOND.
THEN I GUESS I'M STUCK THIS WAY FOREVER.

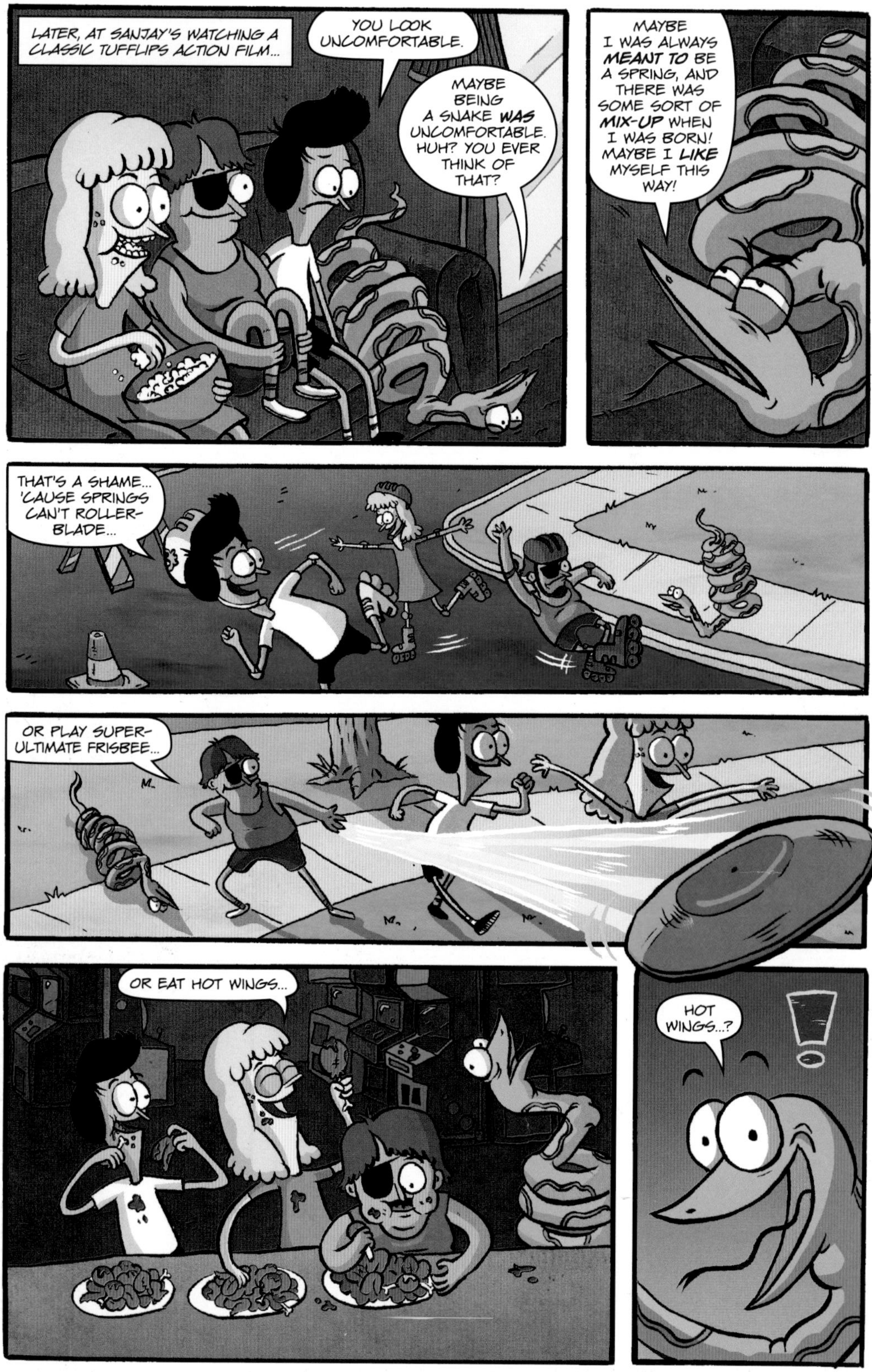
LATER, AT SANJAY'S WATCHING A CLASSIC TUFFLIPS ACTION FILM...
YOU LOOK UNCOMFORTABLE.
MAYBE BEING A SNAKE WAS UNCOMFORTABLE. HUH? YOU EVER THINK OF THAT?
MAYBE I WAS ALWAYS MEANT TO BE A SPRING, AND THERE WAS SOME SORT OF MIX-UP WHEN I WAS BORN! MAYBE I LIKE MYSELF THIS WAY!
THAT'S A SHAME... 'CAUSE SPRINGS CAN'T ROLLER-BLADE...
OR PLAY SUPER-ULTIMATE FRISBEE...
OR EAT HOT WINGS...
HOT WINGS...?
!

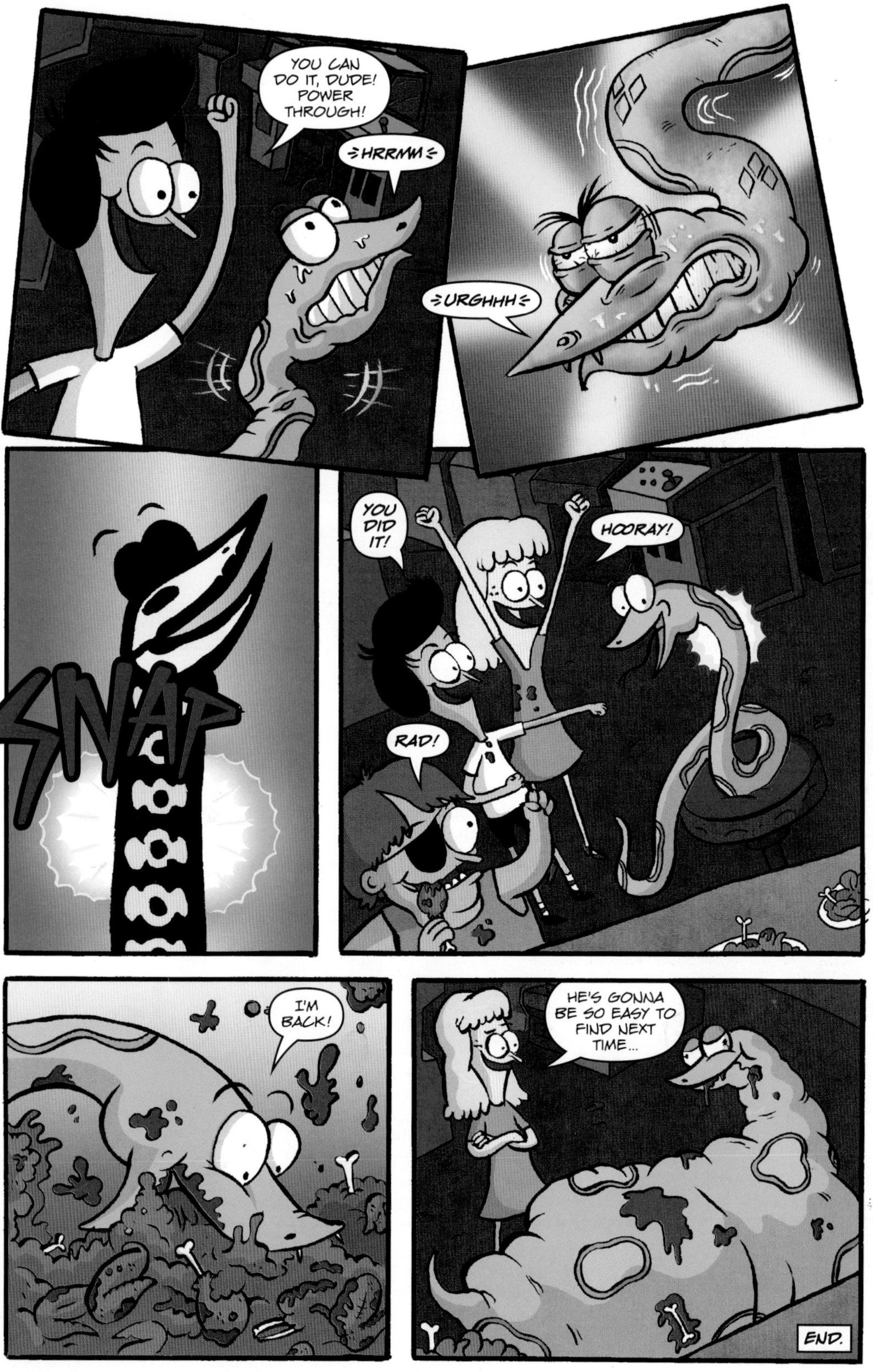
YOU CAN DO IT, DUDE! POWER THROUGH!
HRRMM
URGHHH
SNAP
YOU DID IT!
HOORAY!
RAD!
I'M BACK!
HE'S GONNA BE SO EASY TO FIND NEXT TIME...
END.

Count Tufflips

THE TUFFEST MAN ALIVE

Remington Tufflips is the undisputed grand champion of the butt-kicking arts. After defeating the multiverse's top masters of KUNG-FU, SHADOW BOXING, THUMB WRESTLING, SUDOKU, etc., his Tuffness Count Remington Tufflips III acquired the title of "THE WORLD'S TUFFEST FIGHTING ARTS CHAMPION AND MASTER."

TUFFLIPS

FIGHTING SOCIETY

NOW...THE WORLD'S **TUFFEST FIGHTING SECRETS** CAN BE YOURS!

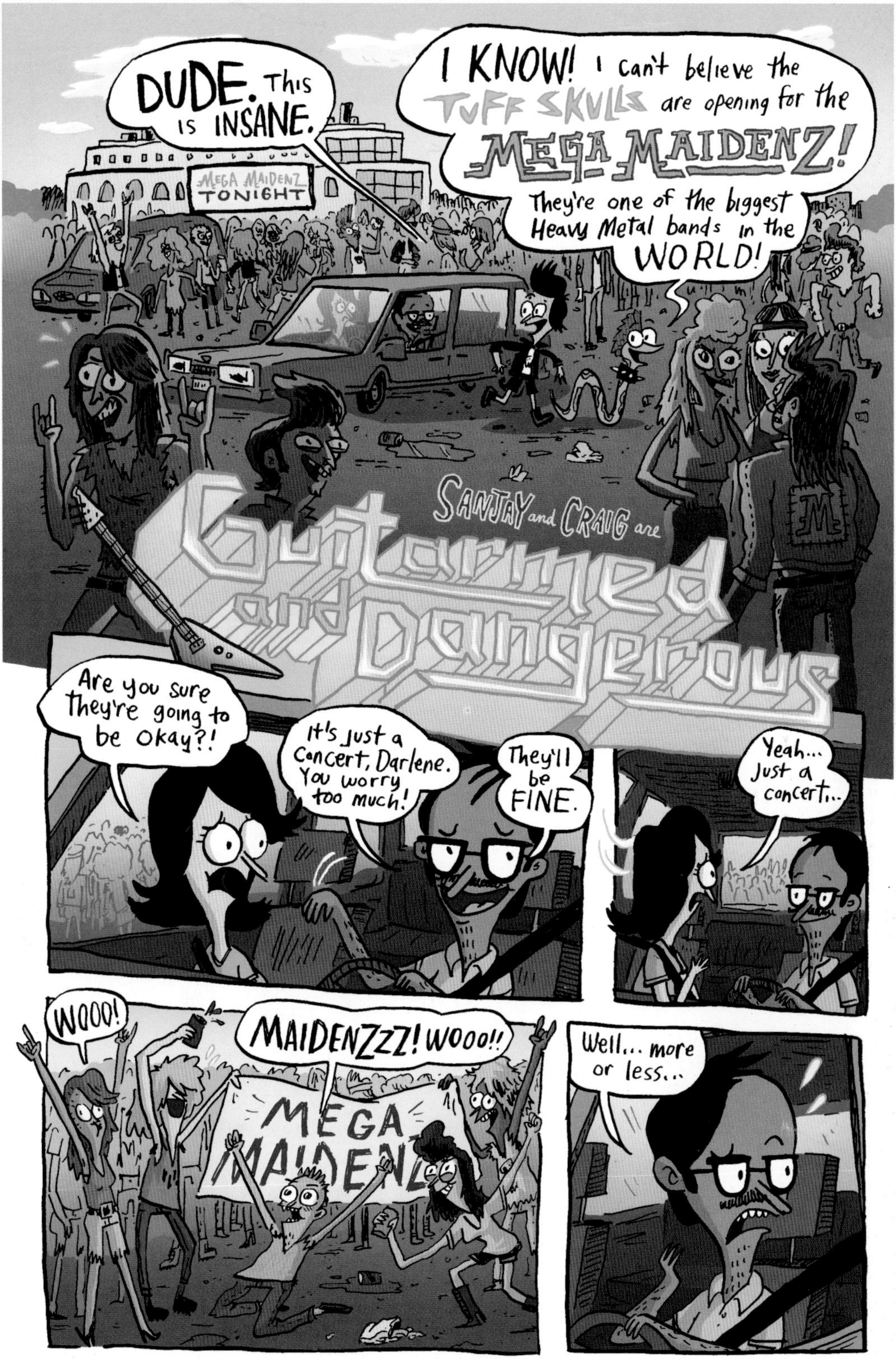
DUDE. This is INSANE.
I KNOW! I can't believe the TUFF SKULLS are opening for the MEGA MAIDENZ!
They're one of the biggest Heavy Metal bands in the WORLD!
MEGA MAIDENZ TONIGHT
SANJAY and CRAIG are Outarmed and Dangerous
Are you sure they're going to be okay?!
It's just a concert, Darlene. You worry too much!
They'll be FINE.
Yeah... Just a concert...
WOOO!
MAIDENZZZ! WOOO!!
MEGA MAIDENZ
Well... more or less...

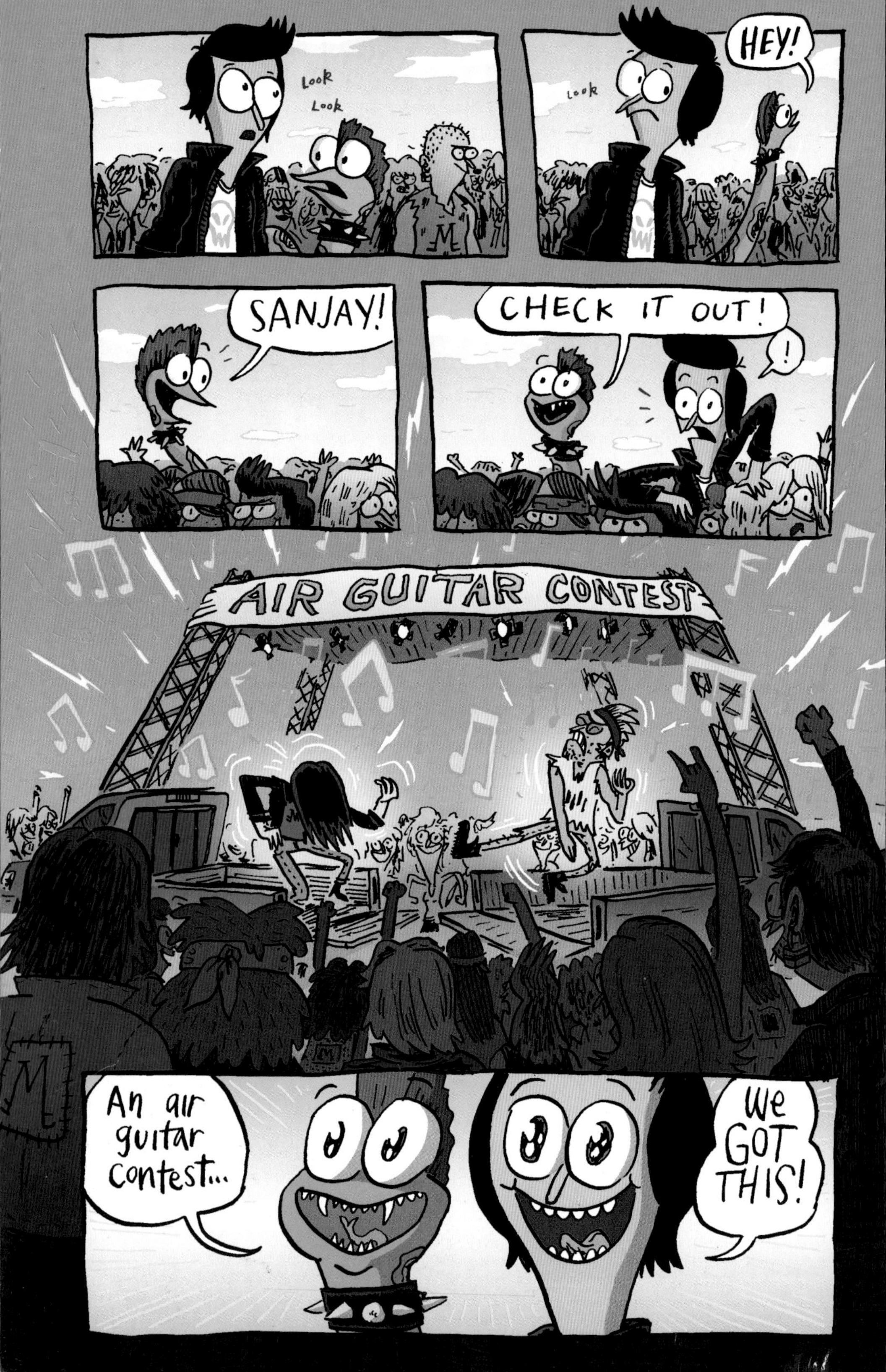
LOOK
LOOK
LOOK
HEY!
SANJAY!
CHECK IT OUT!
!
AIR GUITAR CONTEST
An air guitar contest...
We GOT THIS!

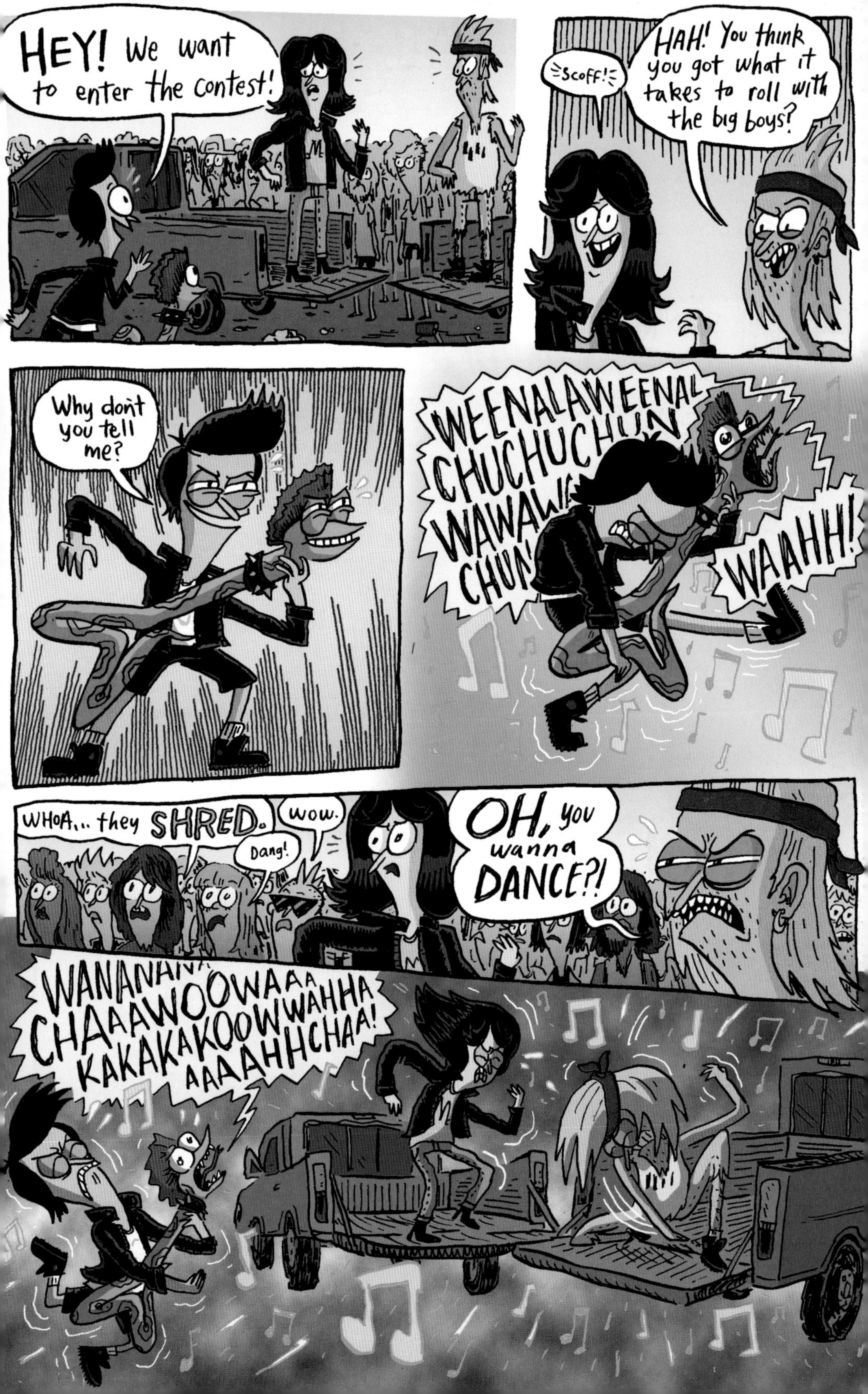
HEY! We want to enter the contest!
Scoff!
HAH! You think you got what it takes to roll with the big boys?
Why don't you tell me?
WEENALAWEENAL CHUCHUCHUN WAWAW CHUN
WAAHH!
WHOA... they SHRED.
wow.
Dang!
OH, you wanna DANCE?!
WANANAN WAAAWOOWAAA CHAAAWOOWWAHHA KAKAKAKOOWWAHHA AAAAHHCHAA!

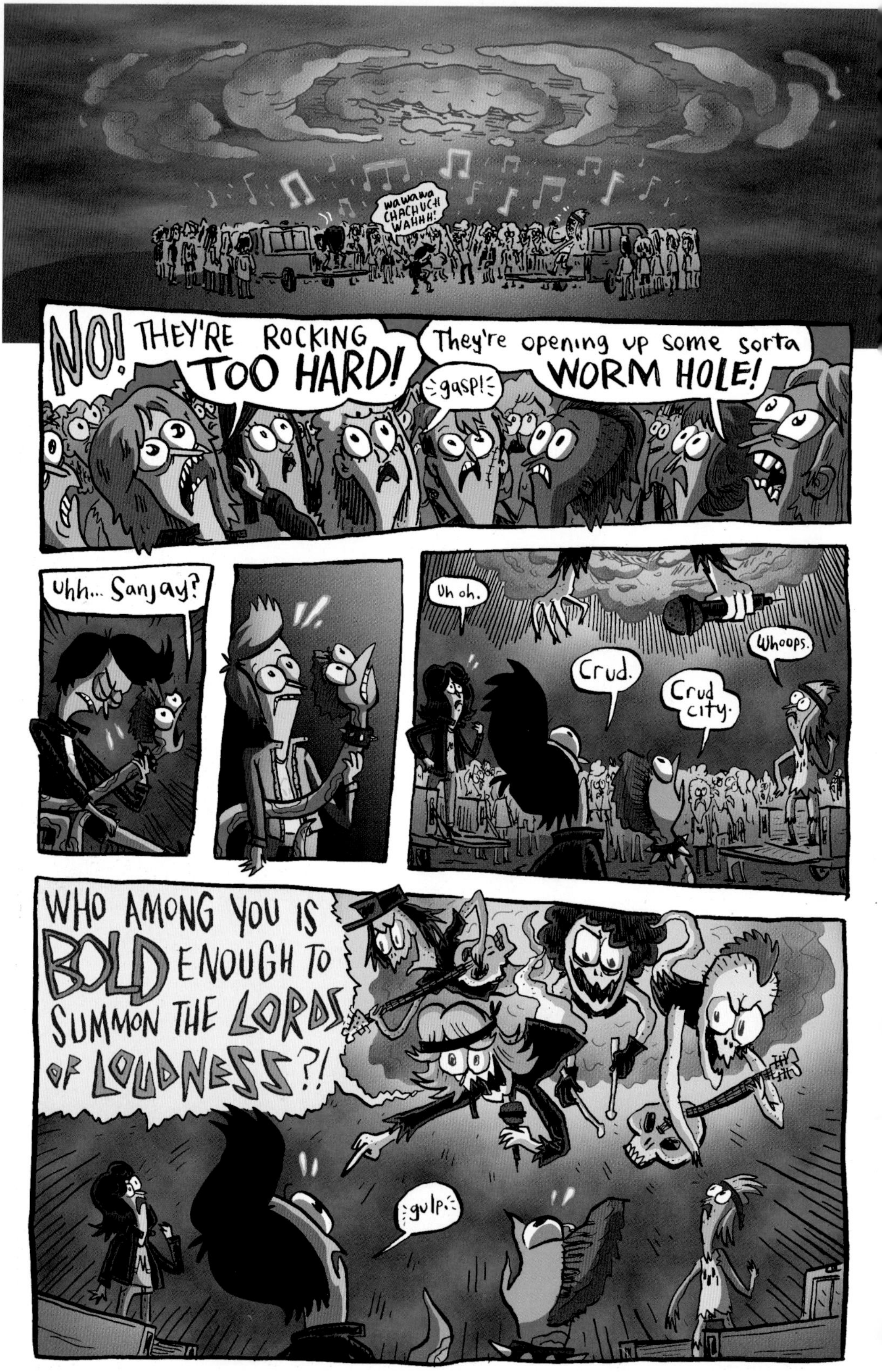
WAWAWA CHACHUCH WAHHH!
NO! THEY'RE ROCKING TOO HARD!
They're opening up some sorta WORM HOLE!
gasp!
Uhh... Sanjay?
Uh oh.
Crud.
Crud city.
Whoops.
WHO AMONG YOU IS BOLD ENOUGH TO SUMMON THE LORDS OF LOUDNESS?!
gulp.

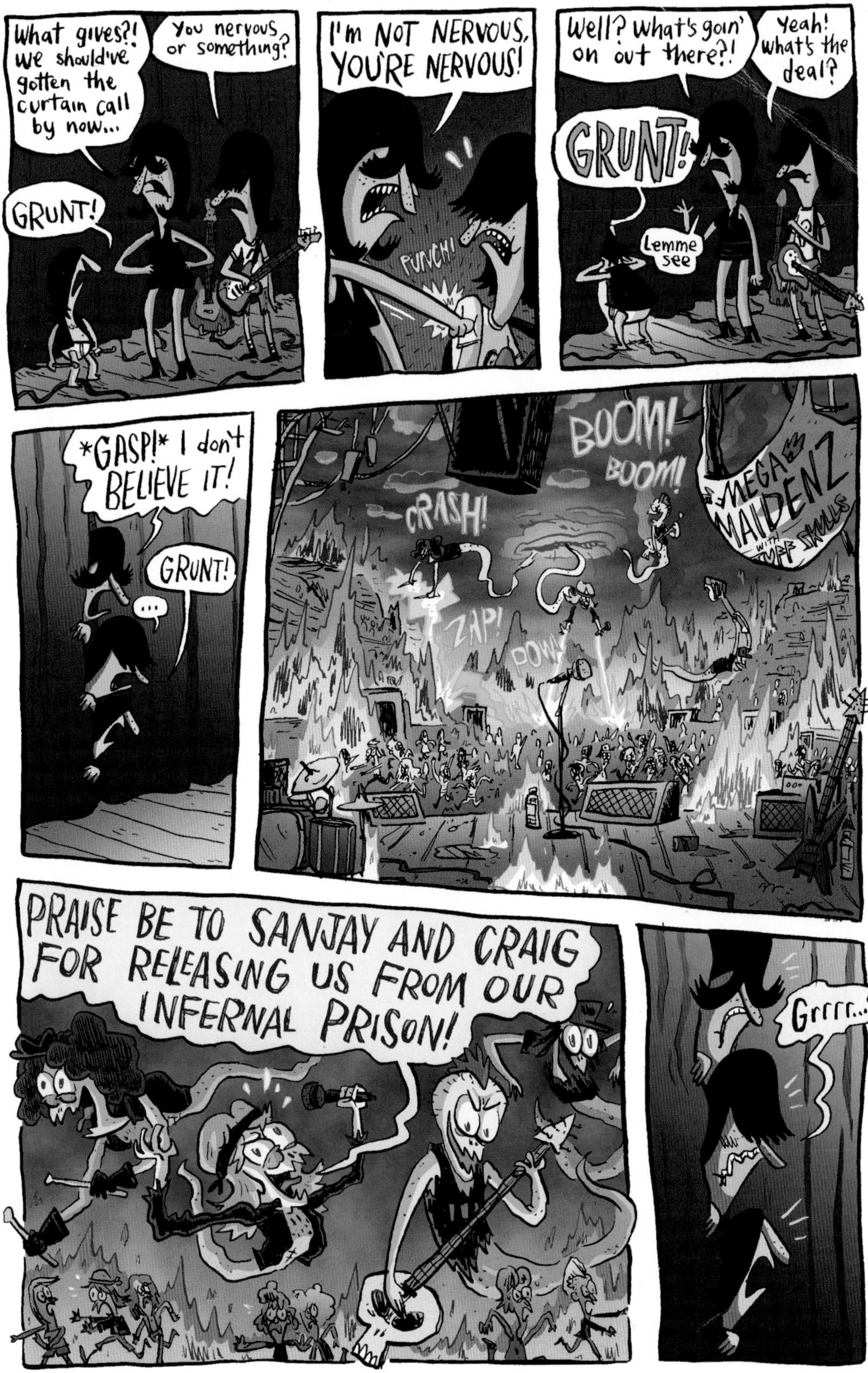
What gives?! we should've gotten the curtain call by now...
You nervous or something?
GRUNT!
I'm NOT NERVOUS, YOU'RE NERVOUS!
PUNCH!
Well? What's goin' on out there?!
Yeah! what's the deal?
GRUNT!
Lemme see
GASP! I don't BELIEVE IT!
GRUNT!
...
BOOM!
BOOM!
MEGA MAIDENZ
WITH TUFF SKULLS
CRASH!
ZAP!
PRAISE BE TO SANJAY AND CRAIG FOR RELEASING US FROM OUR INFERNAL PRISON!
Grrrr...

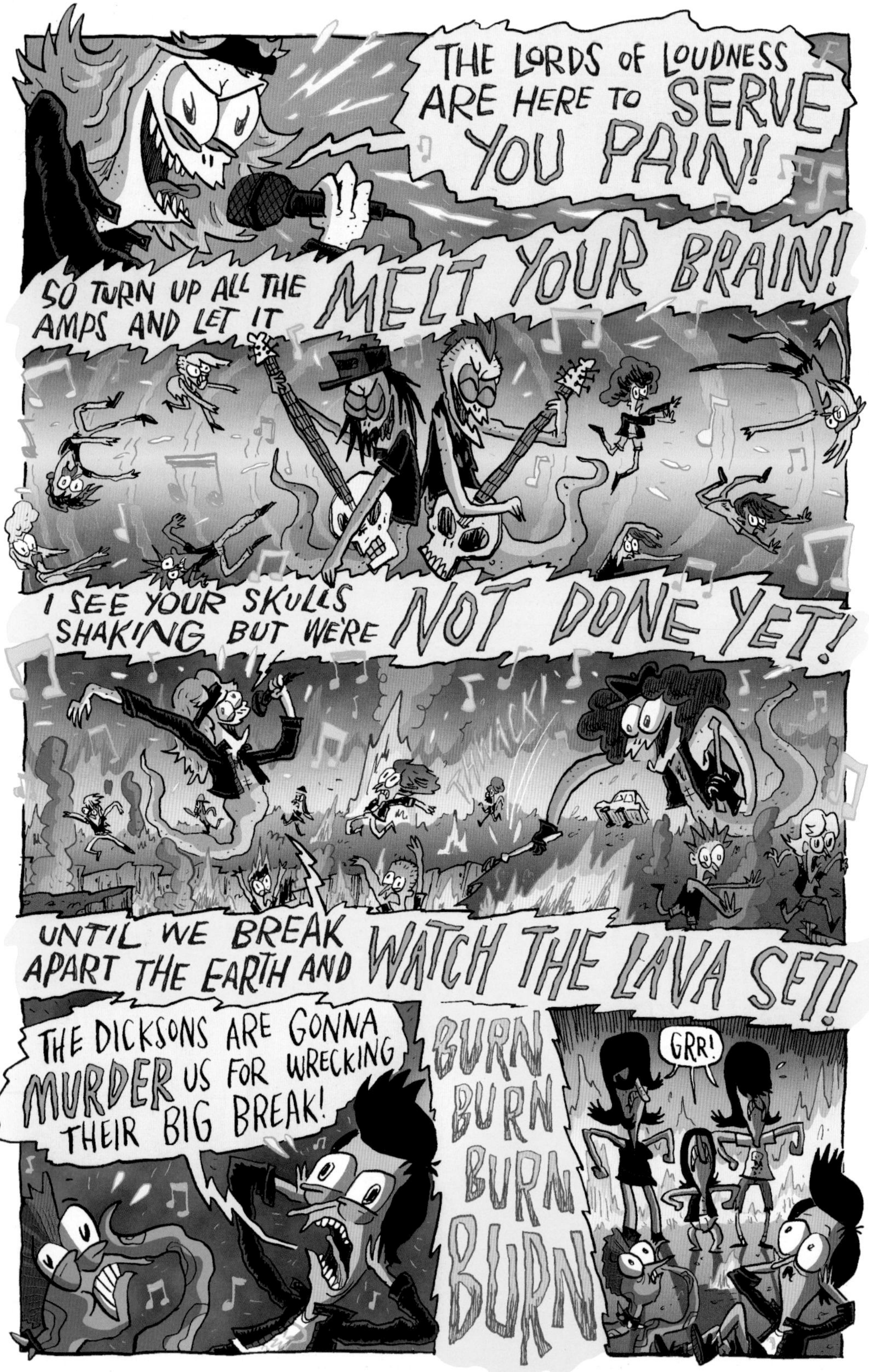
THE LORDS OF LOUDNESS ARE HERE TO SERVE YOU PAIN!
SO TURN UP ALL THE AMPS AND LET IT MELT YOUR BRAIN!
I SEE YOUR SKULLS SHAKING BUT WE'RE NOT DONE YET!
THWACK!
UNTIL WE BREAK APART THE EARTH AND WATCH THE LAVA SET!
THE DICKSONS ARE GONNA MURDER US FOR WRECKING THEIR BIG BREAK!
BURN BURN BURN BURN
GRR!

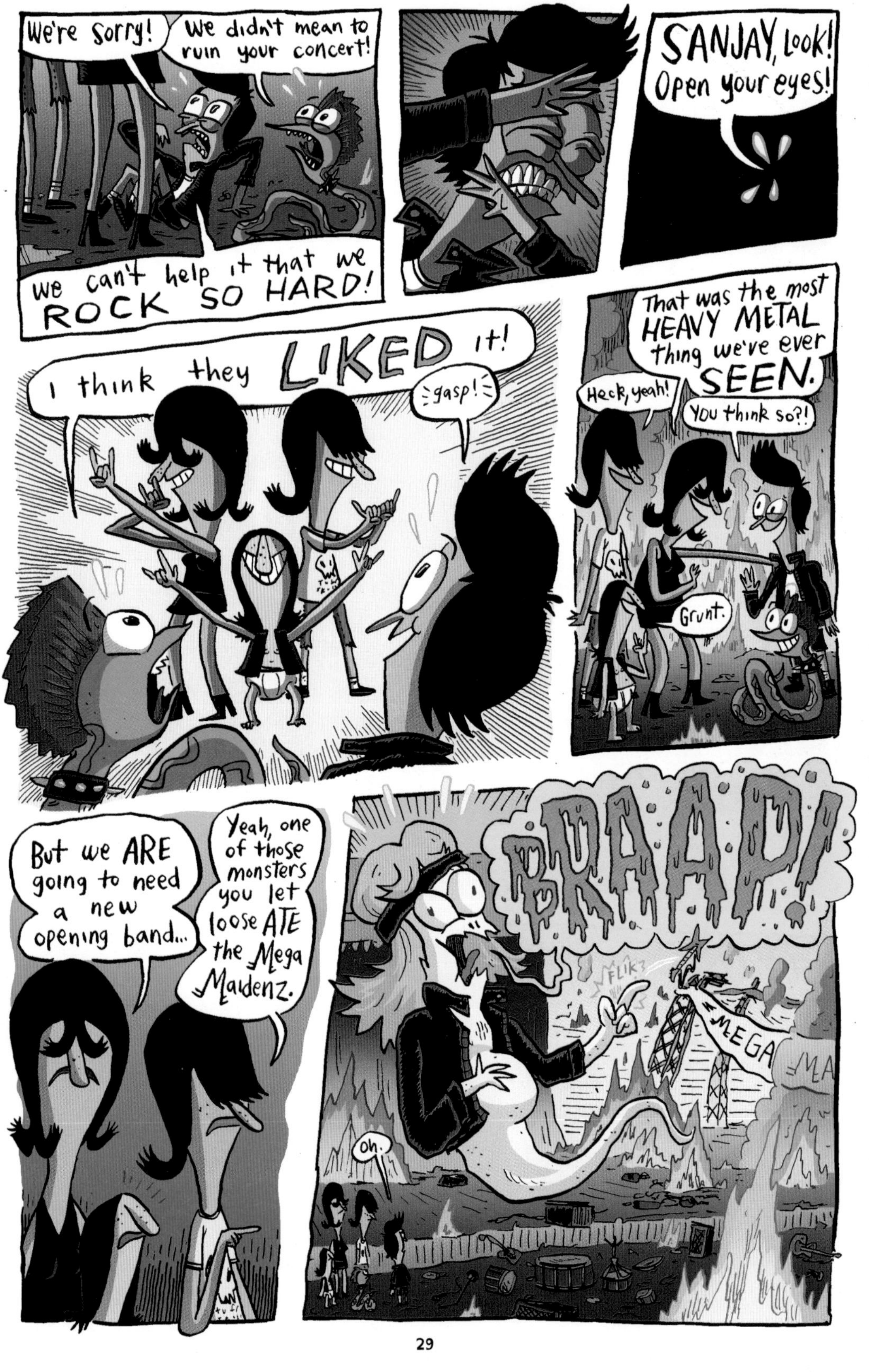
We're sorry!
We didn't mean to ruin your concert!
We can't help it that we ROCK SO HARD!
SANJAY, look! Open your eyes!
I think they LIKED it!
gasp!
That was the most HEAVY METAL thing we've ever SEEN.
Heck, yeah!
You think so?!
Grunt.
But we ARE going to need a new opening band...
Yeah, one of those monsters you let loose ATE the Mega Maidenz.
BRAAP!
FLIK
MEGA
MA
oh.

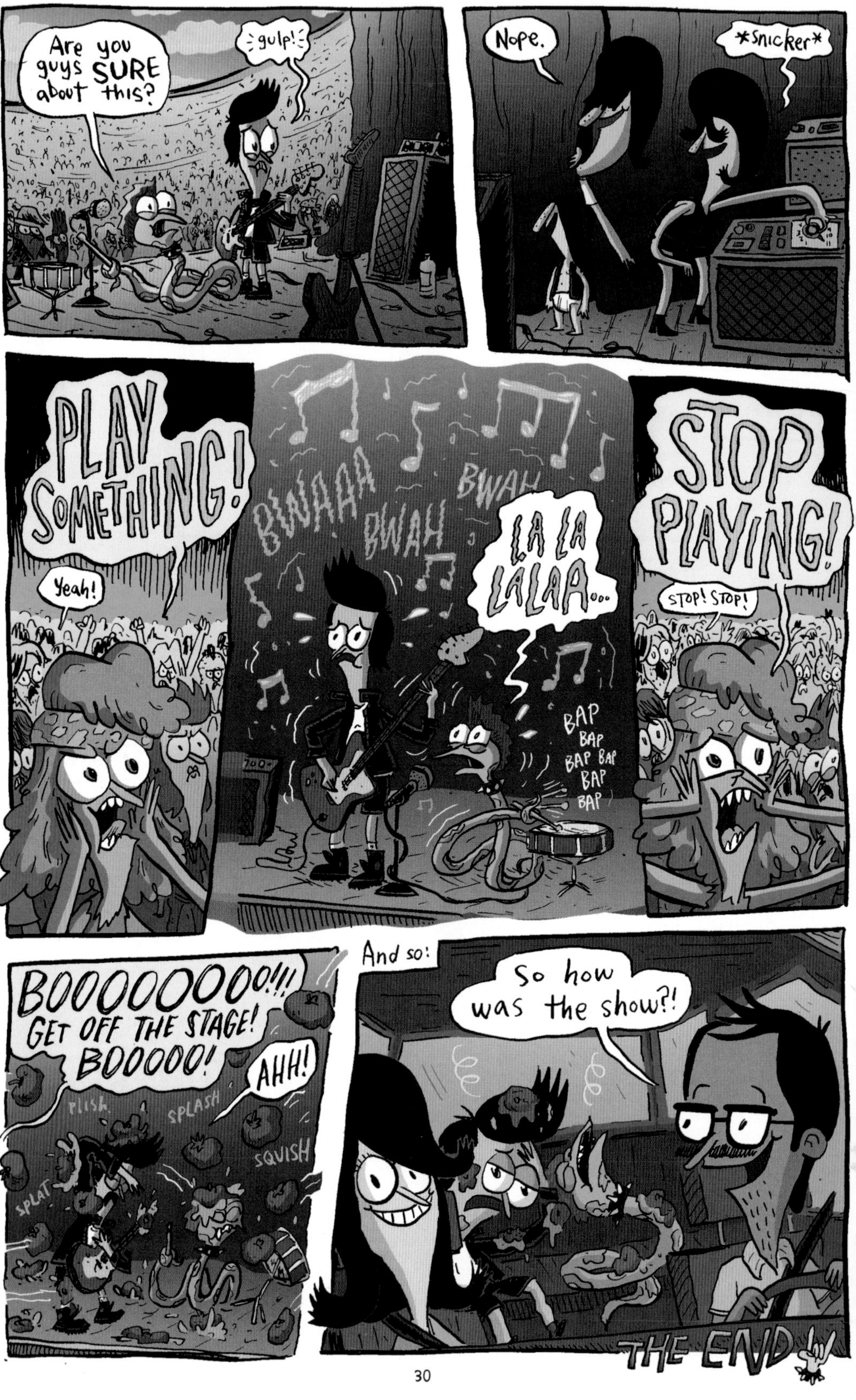
Are you guys SURE about this?
gulp!
Nope.
Snicker
PLAY SOMETHING!
Yeah!
BWAAA BWAH BWAH
LA LA LALAA...
BAP BAP BAP BAP BAP BAP
STOP PLAYING!
STOP! STOP!
BOOOOOOOO!!!
GET OFF THE STAGE!
BOOOOO!
AHH!
PLISH
SPLASH
SQUISH
SPLAT
And so:
So how was the show?!
THE END

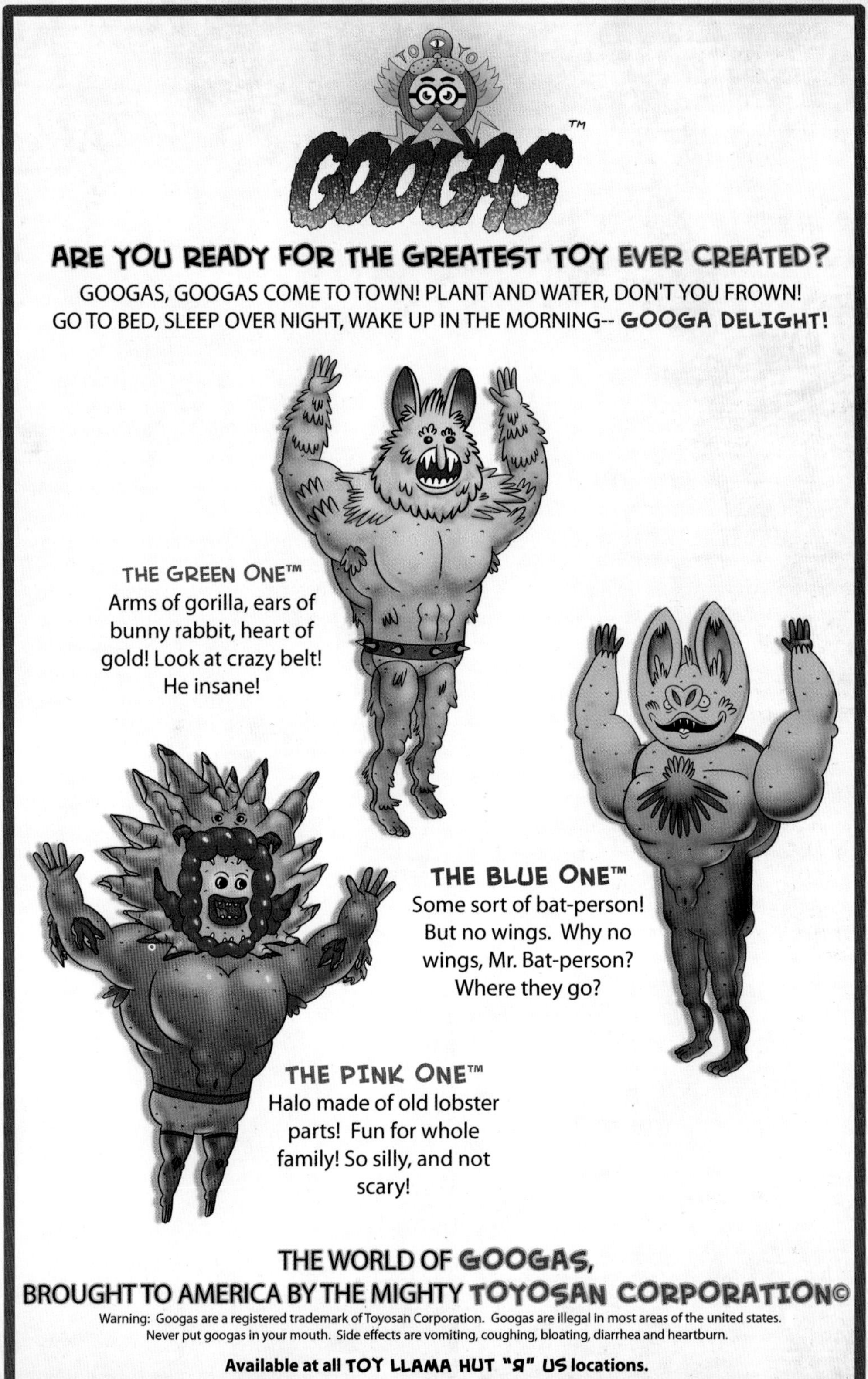

GOOGAS™
ARE YOU READY FOR THE GREATEST TOY EVER CREATED?
GOOGAS, GOOGAS COME TO TOWN! PLANT AND WATER, DON'T YOU FROWN!
GO TO BED, SLEEP OVER NIGHT, WAKE UP IN THE MORNING-- GOOGA DELIGHT!
THE GREEN ONE™
Arms of gorilla, ears of bunny rabbit, heart of gold! Look at crazy belt! He insane!
THE BLUE ONE™
Some sort of bat-person! But no wings. Why no wings, Mr. Bat-person? Where they go?
THE PINK ONE™
Halo made of old lobster parts! Fun for whole family! So silly, and not scary!
THE WORLD OF GOOGAS,
BROUGHT TO AMERICA BY THE MIGHTY TOYOSAN CORPORATION©
Warning: Googas are a registered trademark of Toyosan Corporation. Googas are illegal in most areas of the united states.
Never put googas in your mouth. Side effects are vomiting, coughing, bloating, diarrhea and heartburn.
Available at all TOY LLAMA HUT "Я" US locations.

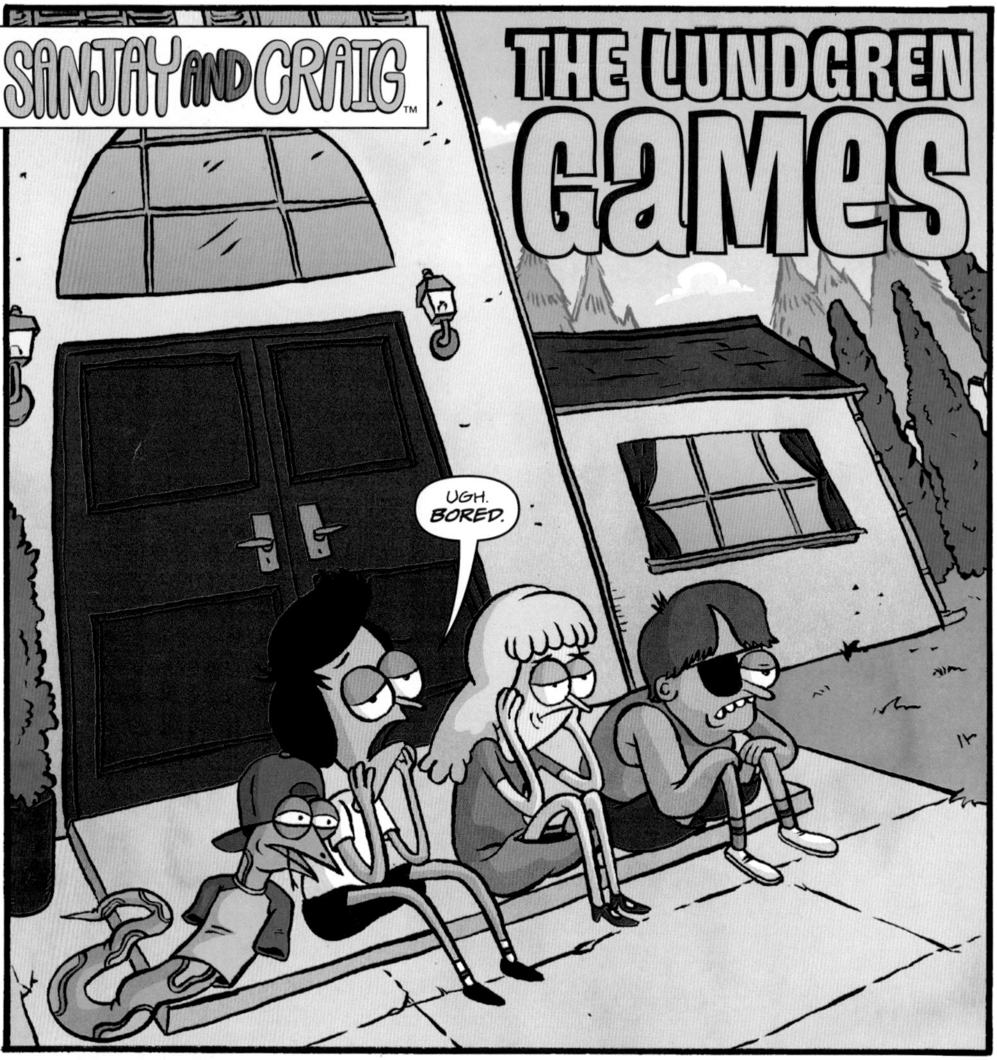
SANJAY AND CRAIG™
THE LUNDGREN GAMES
UGH. BORED.

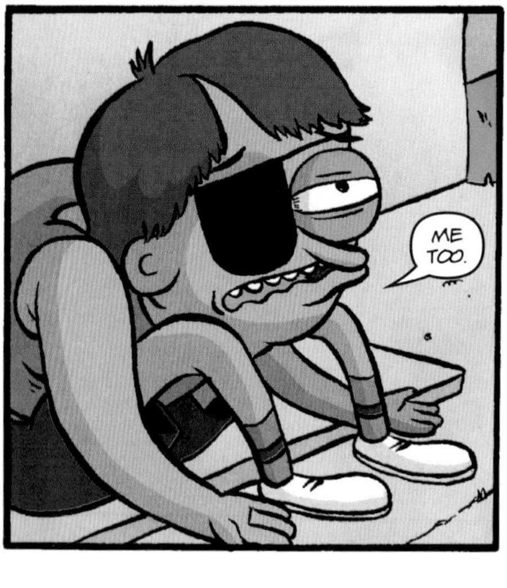
ME TOO.

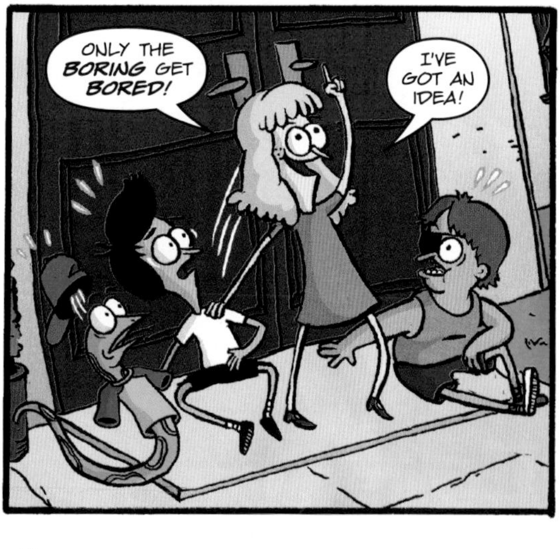
ONLY THE BORING GET BORED!
I'VE GOT AN IDEA!

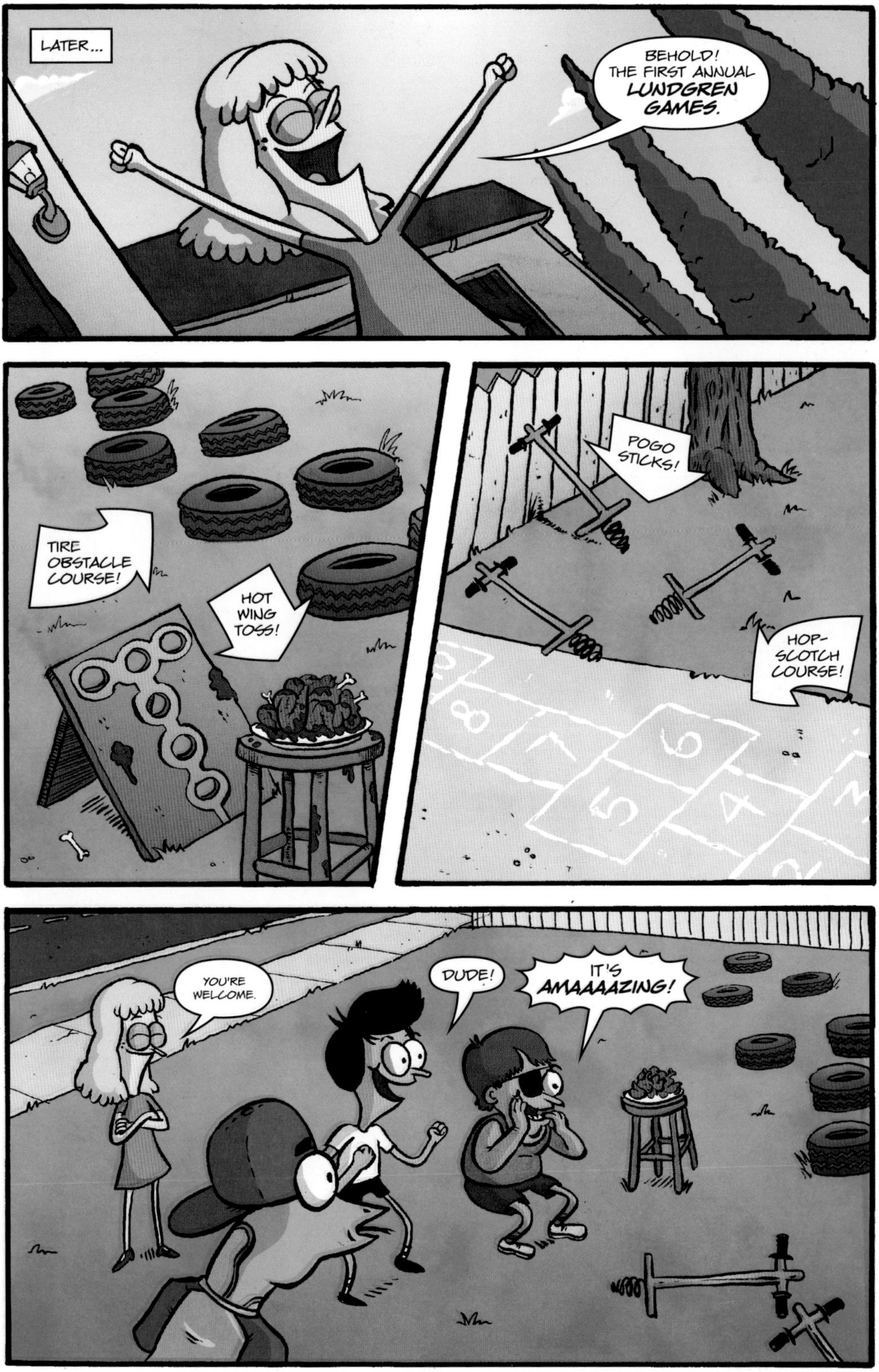
LATER...
BEHOLD! THE FIRST ANNUAL LUNDGREN GAMES.
TIRE OBSTACLE COURSE!
HOT WING TOSS!
POGO STICKS!
HOP-SCOTCH COURSE!
YOU'RE WELCOME.
DUDE!
IT'S AMAAAAZING!

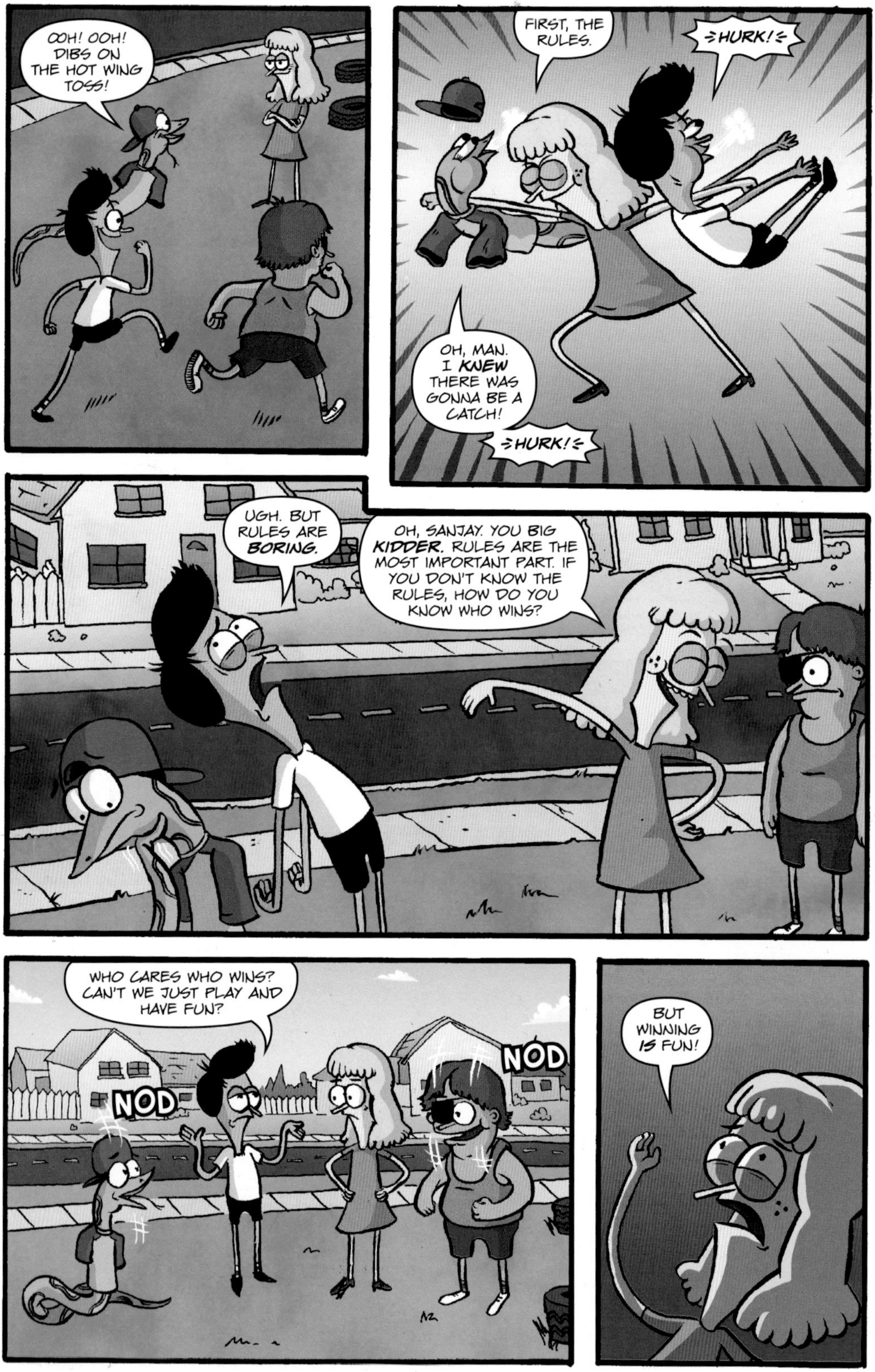
OOH! OOH! DIBS ON THE HOT WING TOSS!
FIRST, THE RULES.
HURK!
OH, MAN. I KNEW THERE WAS GONNA BE A CATCH!
HURK!
UGH. BUT RULES ARE BORING.
OH, SANJAY. YOU BIG KIDDER. RULES ARE THE MOST IMPORTANT PART. IF YOU DON'T KNOW THE RULES, HOW DO YOU KNOW WHO WINS?
WHO CARES WHO WINS? CAN'T WE JUST PLAY AND HAVE FUN?
NOD
NOD
BUT WINNING IS FUN!

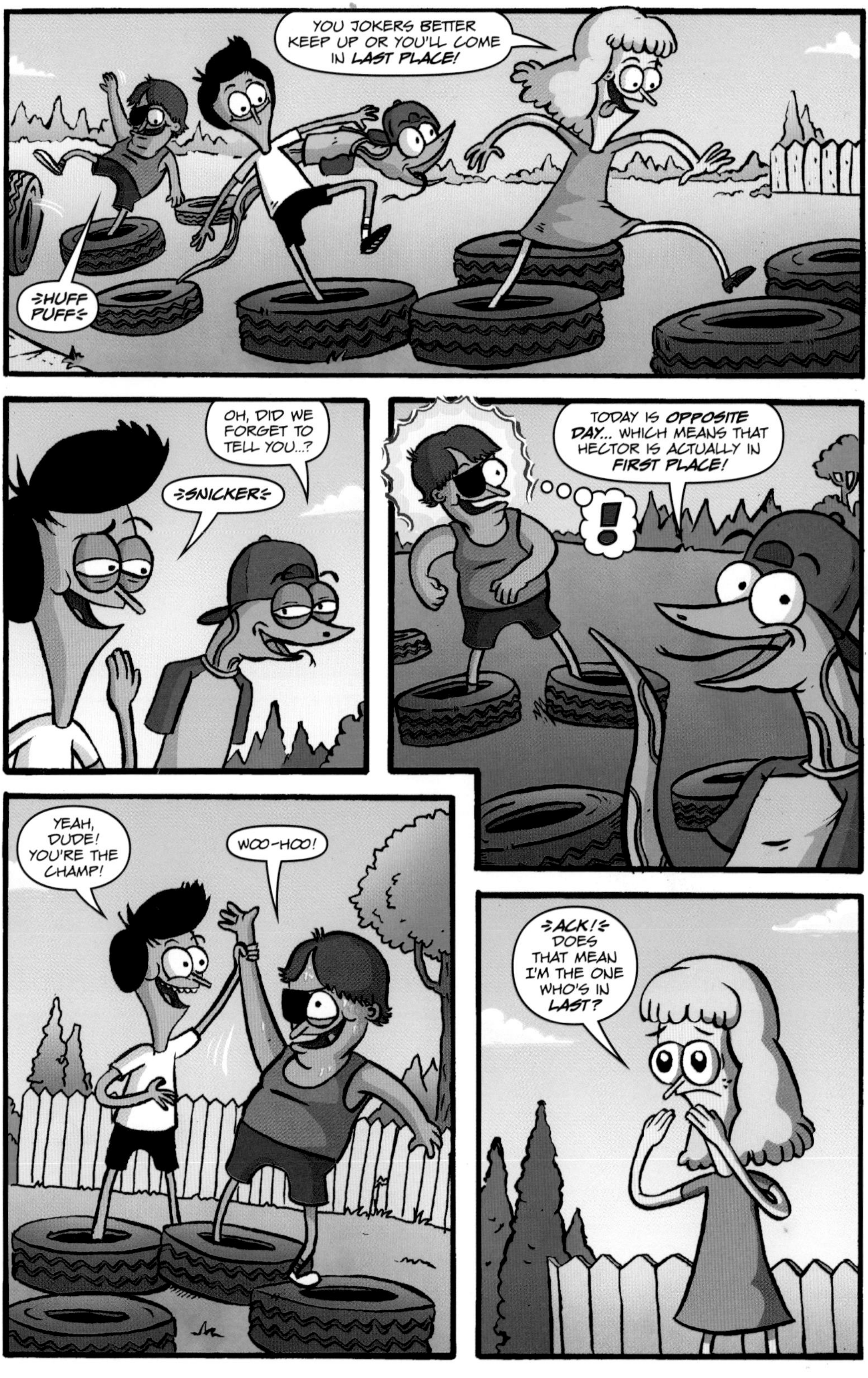
YOU JOKERS BETTER KEEP UP OR YOU'LL COME IN LAST PLACE!
HUFF PUFF
OH, DID WE FORGET TO TELL YOU...?
SNICKER
TODAY IS OPPOSITE DAY... WHICH MEANS THAT HECTOR IS ACTUALLY IN FIRST PLACE!
!
YEAH, DUDE! YOU'RE THE CHAMP!
WOO-HOO!
ACK! DOES THAT MEAN I'M THE ONE WHO'S IN LAST?

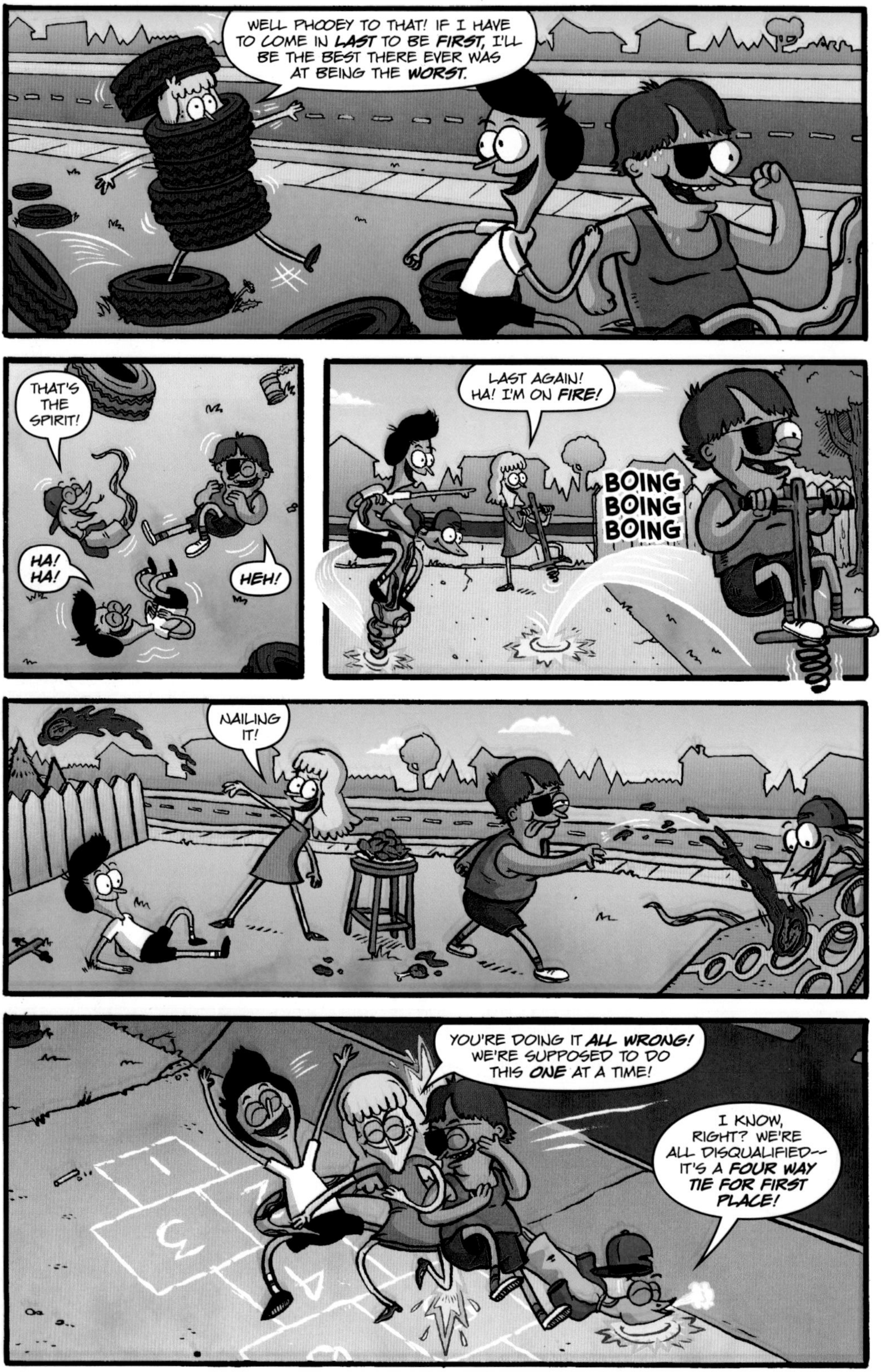
WELL PHOOEY TO THAT! IF I HAVE TO COME IN LAST TO BE FIRST, I'LL BE THE BEST THERE EVER WAS AT BEING THE WORST.
THAT'S THE SPIRIT!
HA! HA!
HEH!
LAST AGAIN! HA! I'M ON FIRE!
BOING BOING BOING
NAILING IT!
YOU'RE DOING IT ALL WRONG! WE'RE SUPPOSED TO DO THIS ONE AT A TIME!
I KNOW, RIGHT? WE'RE ALL DISQUALIFIED-- IT'S A FOUR WAY TIE FOR FIRST PLACE!

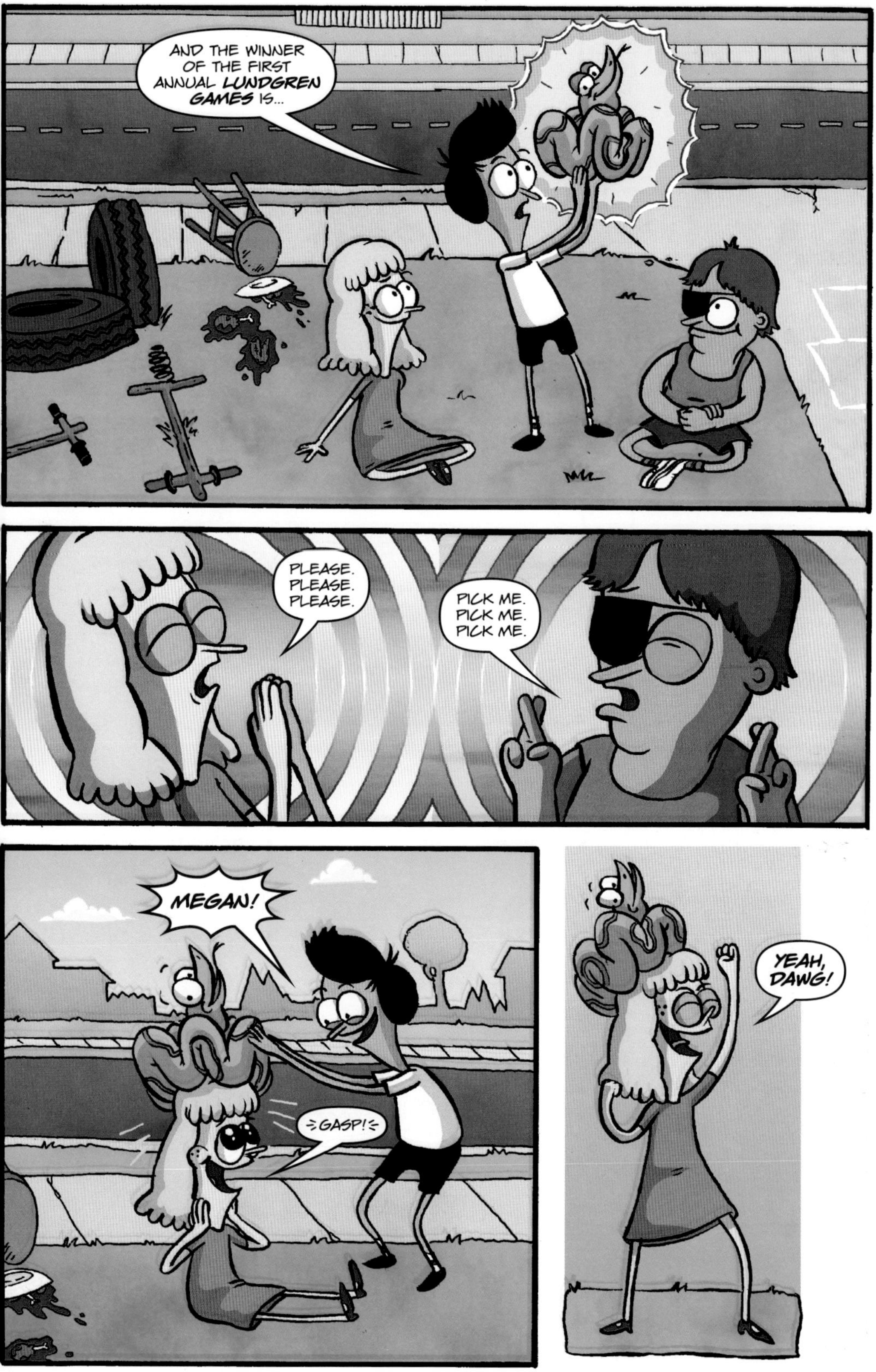
AND THE WINNER OF THE FIRST ANNUAL LUNDGREN GAMES IS...
PLEASE. PLEASE. PLEASE.
PICK ME. PICK ME. PICK ME.
MEGAN!
GASP!
YEAH, DAWG!

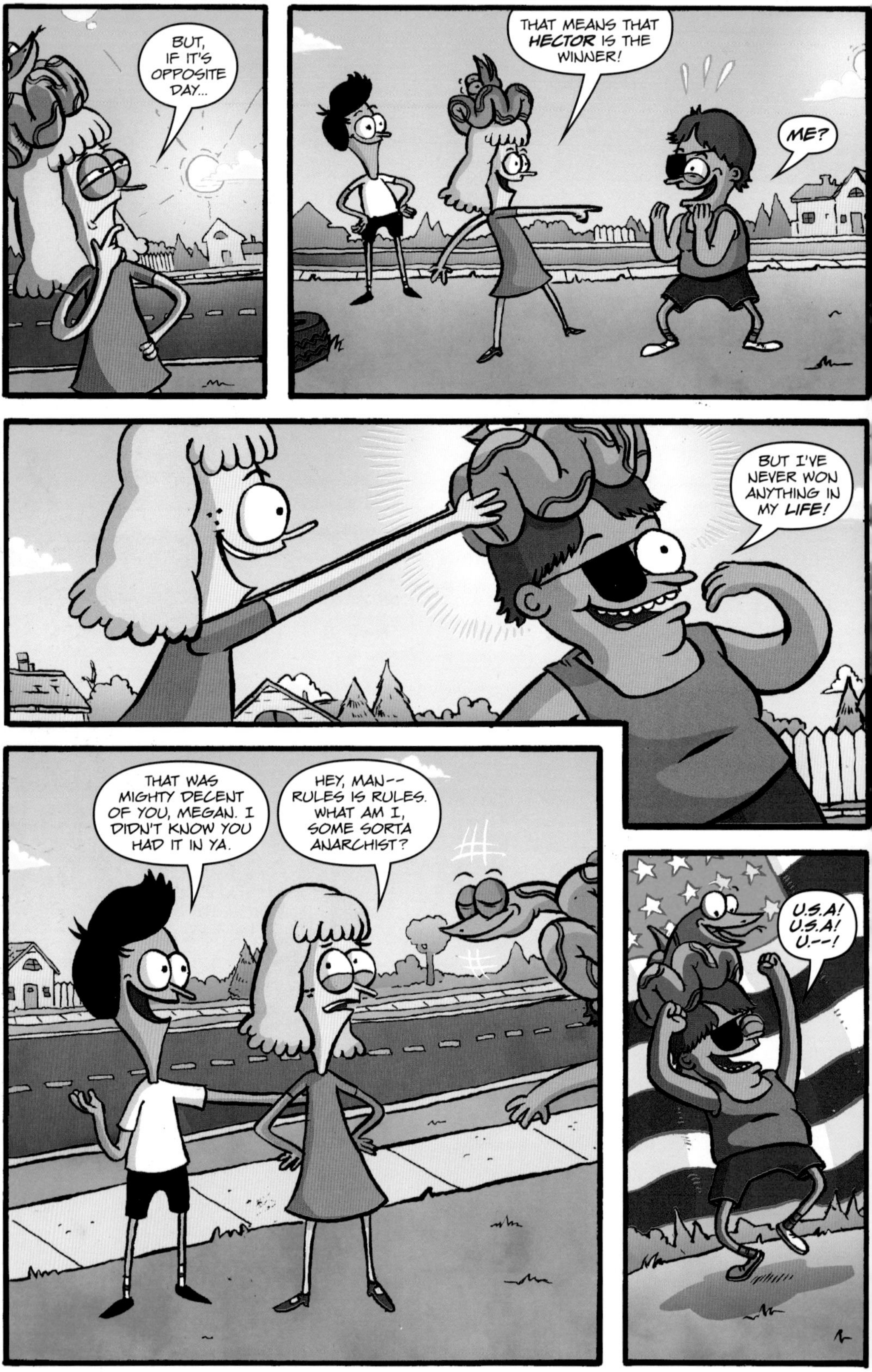
BUT, IF IT'S OPPOSITE DAY...
THAT MEANS THAT **HECTOR** IS THE WINNER!
ME?
BUT I'VE NEVER WON ANYTHING IN MY **LIFE!**
THAT WAS MIGHTY DECENT OF YOU, MEGAN. I DIDN'T KNOW YOU HAD IT IN YA.
HEY, MAN-- RULES IS RULES. WHAT AM I, SOME SORTA ANARCHIST?
U.S.A! U.S.A! U.--!

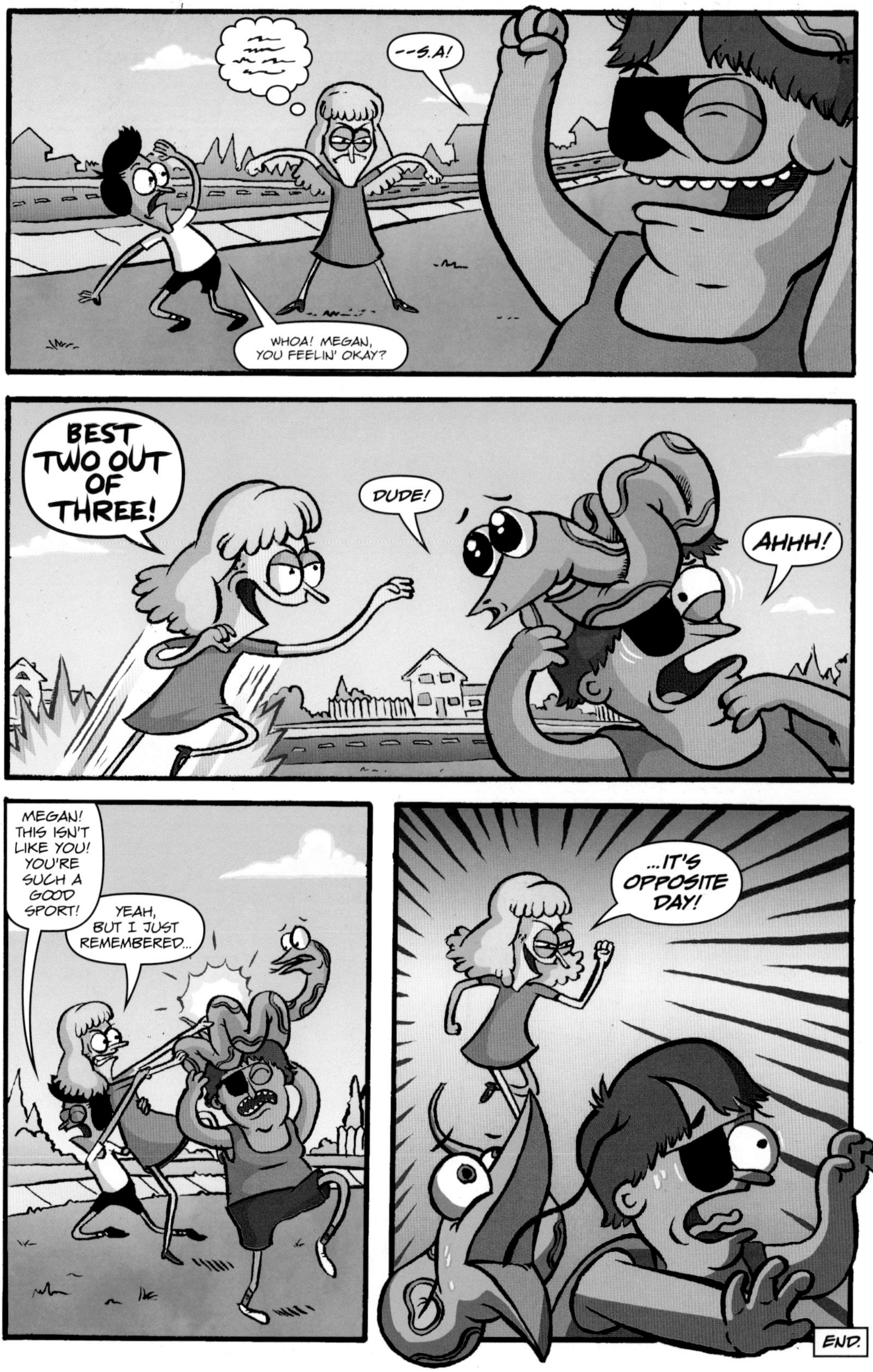
--S.A!
WHOA! MEGAN, YOU FEELIN' OKAY?
BEST TWO OUT OF THREE!
DUDE!
AHHH!
MEGAN! THIS ISN'T LIKE YOU! YOU'RE SUCH A GOOD SPORT!
YEAH, BUT I JUST REMEMBERED...
...IT'S OPPOSITE DAY!
END.

SANJAY AND CRAIG™ ULTIMATE CRYING CHAMPIONSHIP

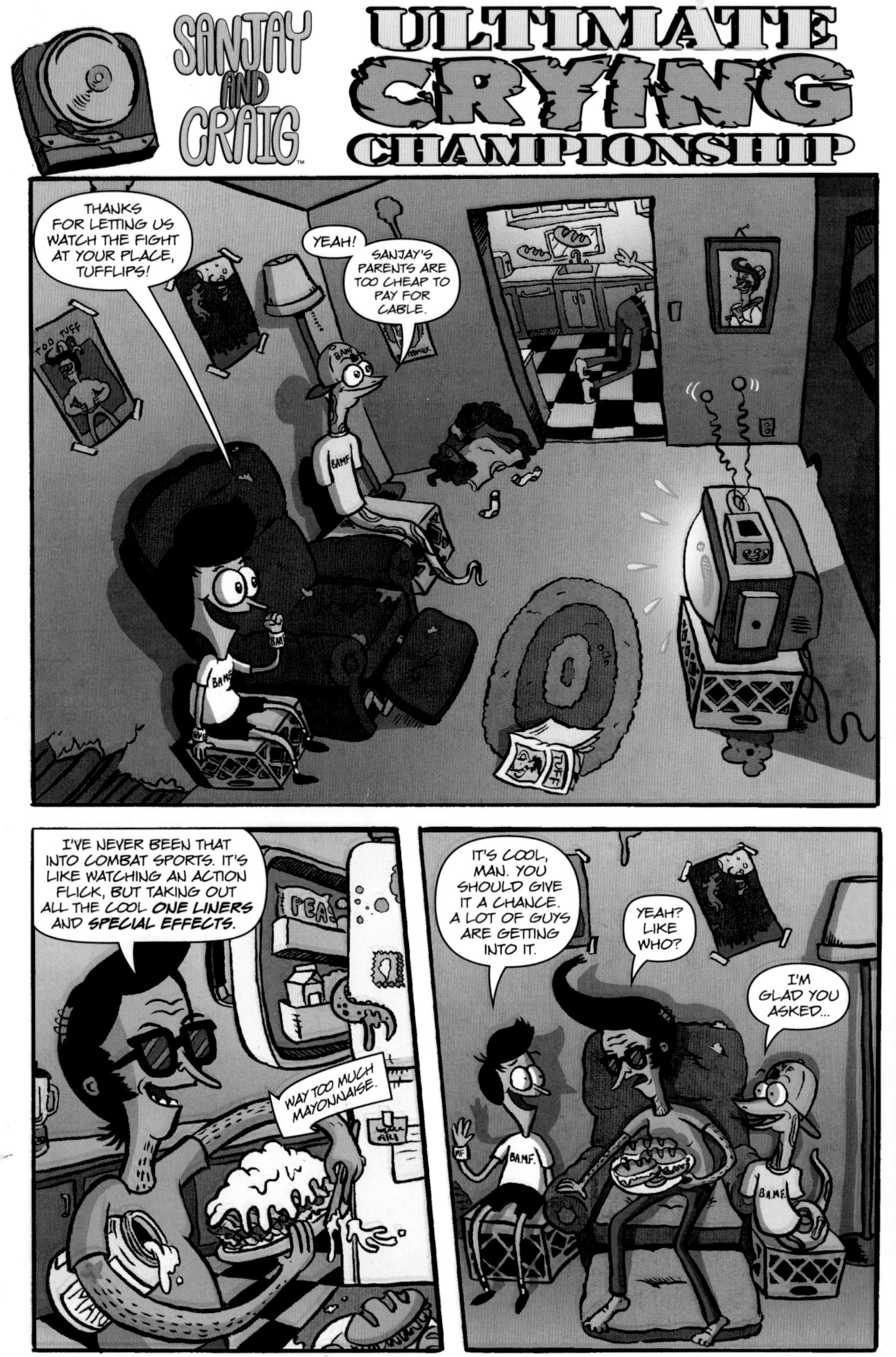

THANKS FOR LETTING US WATCH THE FIGHT AT YOUR PLACE, TUFFLIPS!
YEAH!
SANJAY'S PARENTS ARE TOO CHEAP TO PAY FOR CABLE.
TOO TUFF
TUFF
I'VE NEVER BEEN THAT INTO COMBAT SPORTS. IT'S LIKE WATCHING AN ACTION FLICK, BUT TAKING OUT ALL THE COOL ONE LINERS AND SPECIAL EFFECTS.
PEAS
WAY TOO MUCH MAYONNAISE.
IT'S COOL, MAN. YOU SHOULD GIVE IT A CHANCE. A LOT OF GUYS ARE GETTING INTO IT.
YEAH? LIKE WHO?
I'M GLAD YOU ASKED...

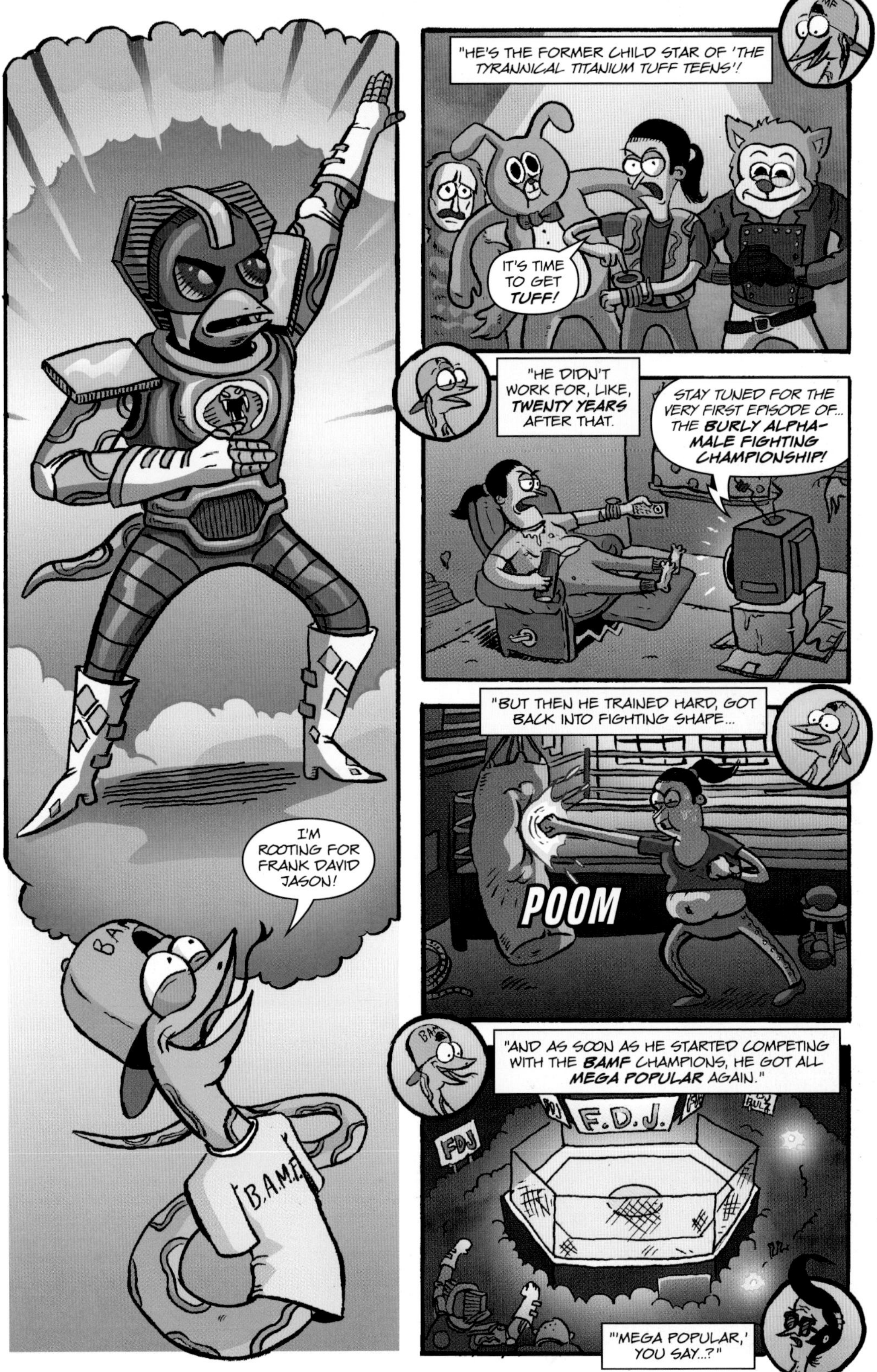

I'M ROOTING FOR FRANK DAVID JASON!
B.A.M.F.
"HE'S THE FORMER CHILD STAR OF 'THE TYRANNICAL TITANIUM TUFF TEENS'!
IT'S TIME TO GET TUFF!
"HE DIDN'T WORK FOR, LIKE, TWENTY YEARS AFTER THAT.
STAY TUNED FOR THE VERY FIRST EPISODE OF... THE BURLY ALPHA-MALE FIGHTING CHAMPIONSHIP!
"BUT THEN HE TRAINED HARD, GOT BACK INTO FIGHTING SHAPE...
POOM
"AND AS SOON AS HE STARTED COMPETING WITH THE BAMF CHAMPIONS, HE GOT ALL MEGA POPULAR AGAIN."
F.D.J.
FDJ
"'MEGA POPULAR,' YOU SAY...?"

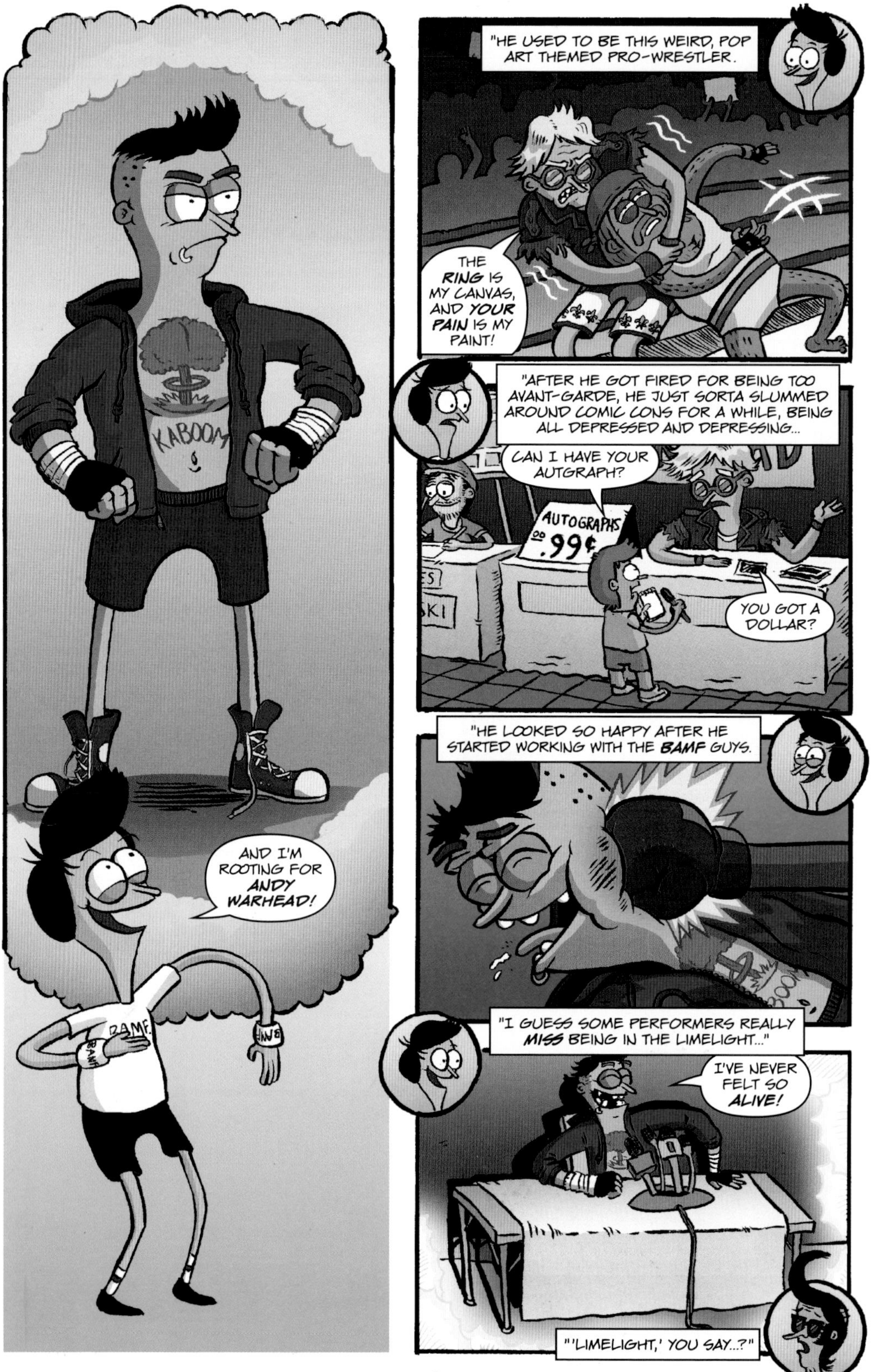

KABOOM
AND I'M ROOTING FOR ANDY WARHEAD!
BAMF
"HE USED TO BE THIS WEIRD, POP ART THEMED PRO-WRESTLER.
THE RING IS MY CANVAS, AND YOUR PAIN IS MY PAINT!
"AFTER HE GOT FIRED FOR BEING TOO AVANT-GARDE, HE JUST SORTA SLUMMED AROUND COMIC CONS FOR A WHILE, BEING ALL DEPRESSED AND DEPRESSING...
CAN I HAVE YOUR AUTGRAPH?
AUTOGRAPHS .99¢
YOU GOT A DOLLAR?
"HE LOOKED SO HAPPY AFTER HE STARTED WORKING WITH THE BAMF GUYS.
"I GUESS SOME PERFORMERS REALLY MISS BEING IN THE LIMELIGHT..."
I'VE NEVER FELT SO ALIVE!
"'LIMELIGHT,' YOU SAY...?"

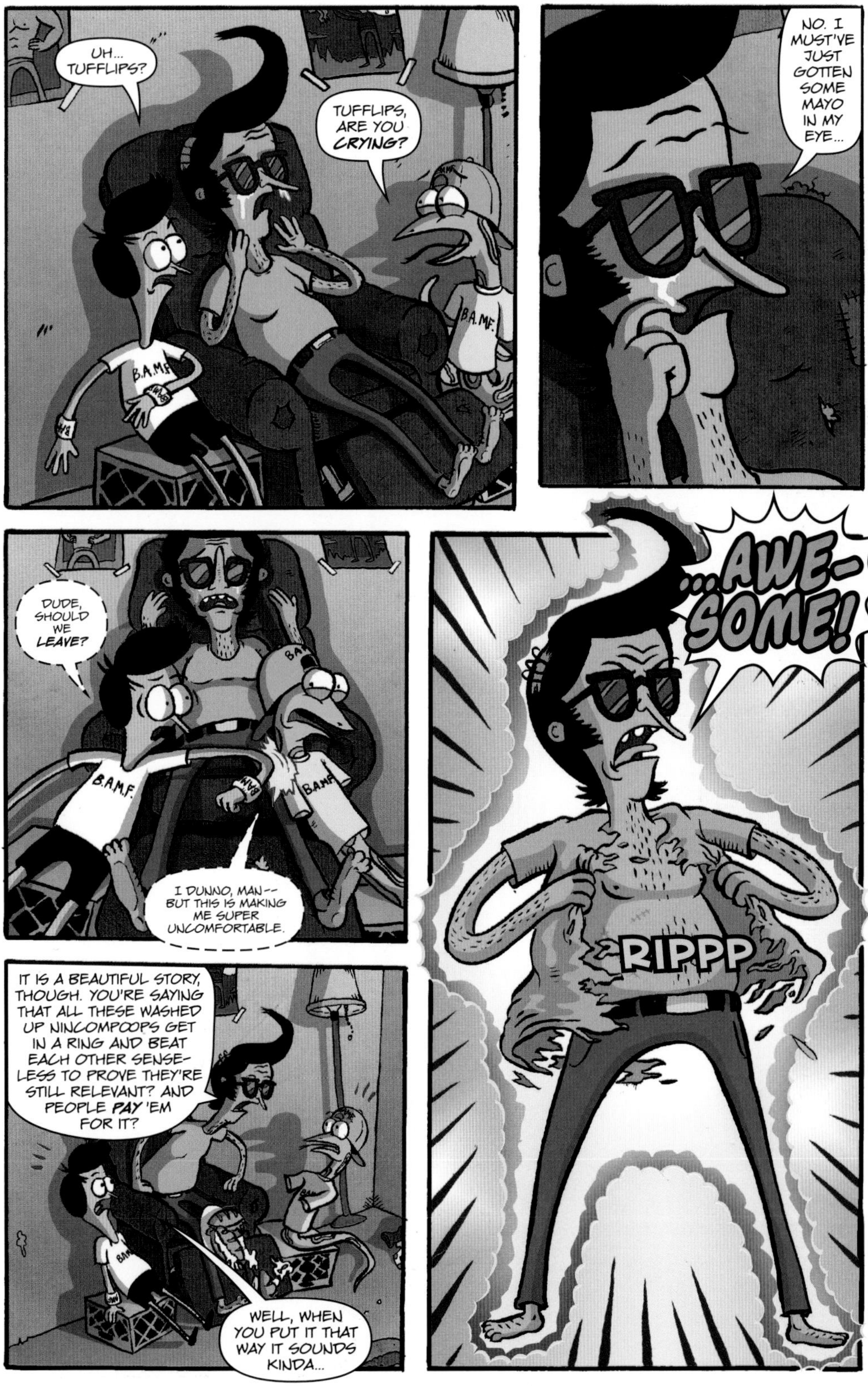

UH... TUFFLIPS?
TUFFLIPS, ARE YOU CRYING?
NO. I MUST'VE JUST GOTTEN SOME MAYO IN MY EYE...
DUDE, SHOULD WE LEAVE?
I DUNNO, MAN-- BUT THIS IS MAKING ME SUPER UNCOMFORTABLE.
IT IS A BEAUTIFUL STORY, THOUGH. YOU'RE SAYING THAT ALL THESE WASHED UP NINCOMPOOPS GET IN A RING AND BEAT EACH OTHER SENSE-LESS TO PROVE THEY'RE STILL RELEVANT? AND PEOPLE PAY 'EM FOR IT?
WELL, WHEN YOU PUT IT THAT WAY IT SOUNDS KINDA...
...AWE-SOME!
RIPPP

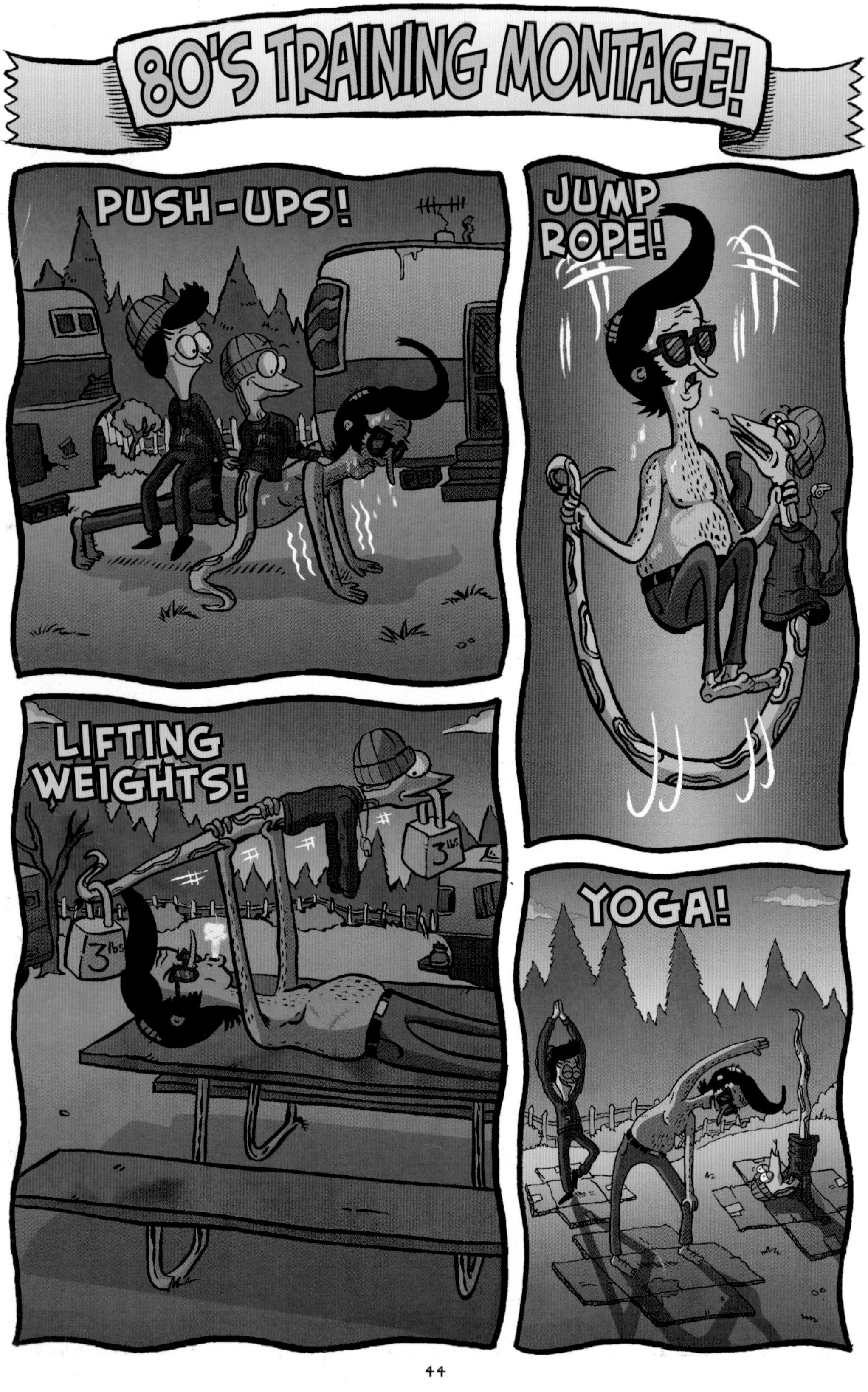
80'S TRAINING MONTAGE!
PUSH-UPS!
JUMP ROPE!
LIFTING WEIGHTS!
3lbs
3lbs
YOGA!

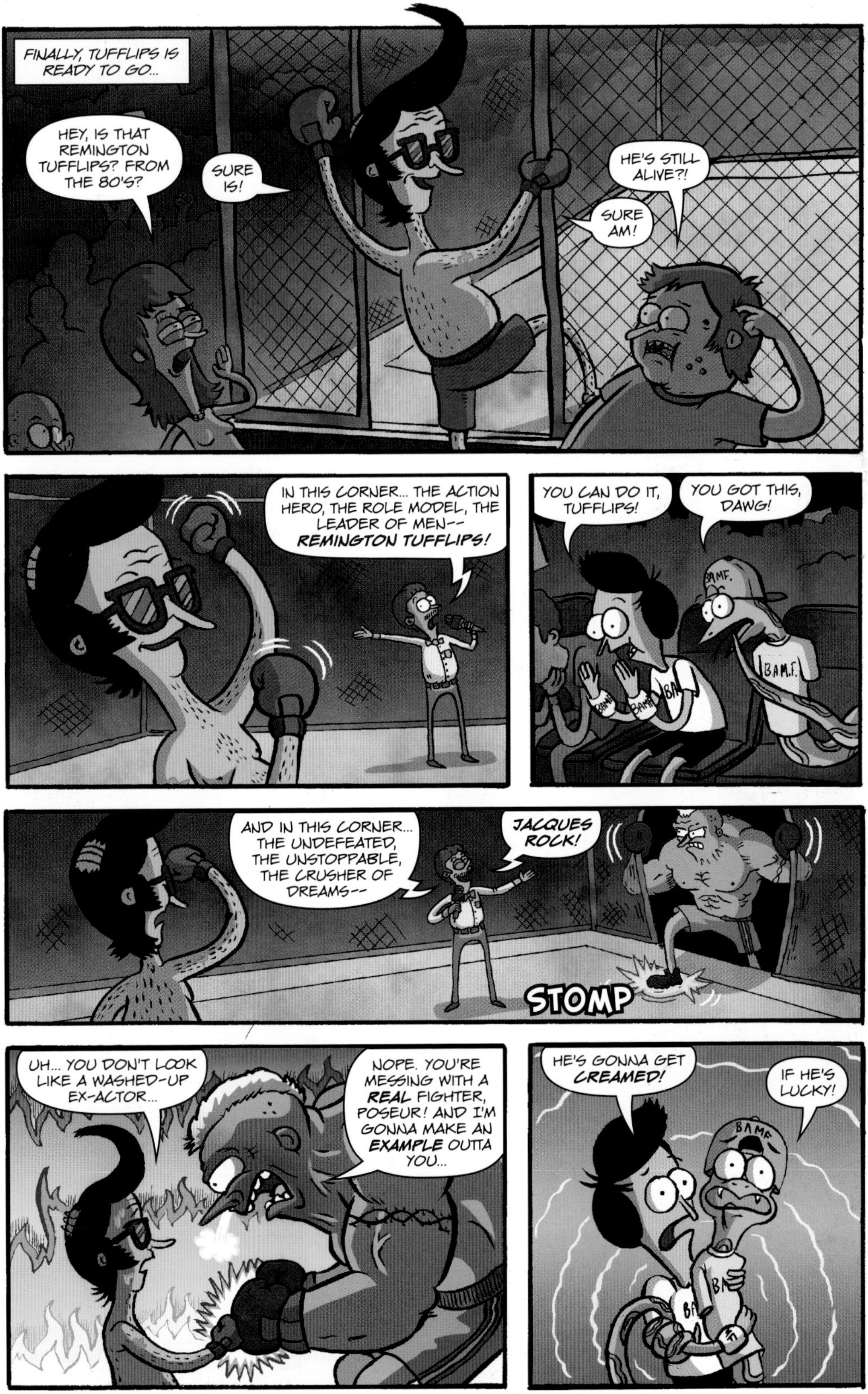

FINALLY, TUFFLIPS IS READY TO GO...
HEY, IS THAT REMINGTON TUFFLIPS? FROM THE 80'S?
SURE IS!
HE'S STILL ALIVE?!
SURE AM!
IN THIS CORNER... THE ACTION HERO, THE ROLE MODEL, THE LEADER OF MEN-- REMINGTON TUFFLIPS!
YOU CAN DO IT, TUFFLIPS!
YOU GOT THIS, DAWG!
AND IN THIS CORNER... THE UNDEFEATED, THE UNSTOPPABLE, THE CRUSHER OF DREAMS--
JACQUES ROCK!
STOMP
UH... YOU DON'T LOOK LIKE A WASHED-UP EX-ACTOR...
NOPE. YOU'RE MESSING WITH A REAL FIGHTER, POSEUR! AND I'M GONNA MAKE AN EXAMPLE OUTTA YOU...
HE'S GONNA GET CREAMED!
IF HE'S LUCKY!

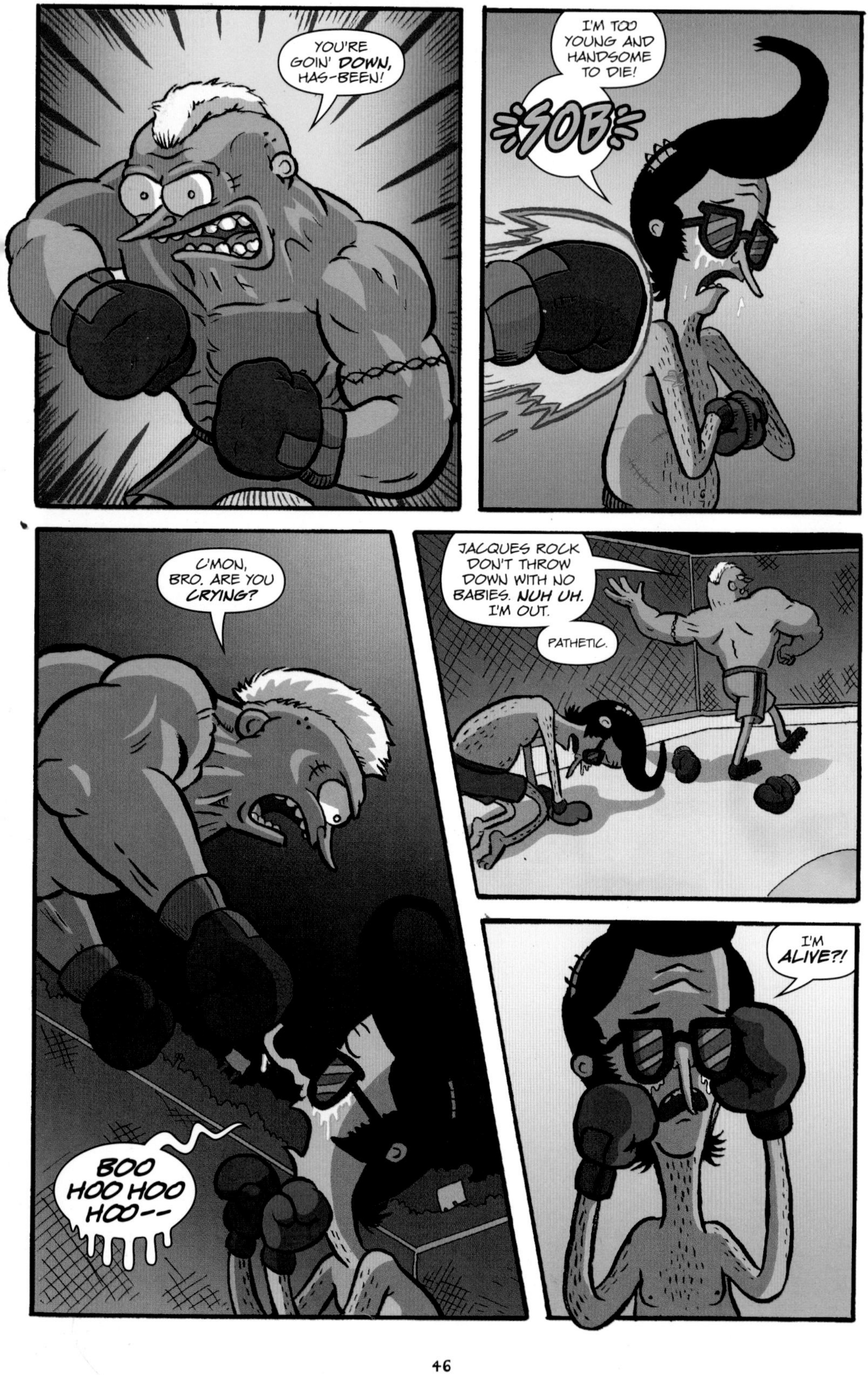
YOU'RE GOIN' DOWN, HAS-BEEN!
I'M TOO YOUNG AND HANDSOME TO DIE!
SOB
C'MON, BRO. ARE YOU CRYING?
BOO HOO HOO HOO--
JACQUES ROCK DON'T THROW DOWN WITH NO BABIES. NUH UH. I'M OUT.
PATHETIC.
I'M ALIVE?!

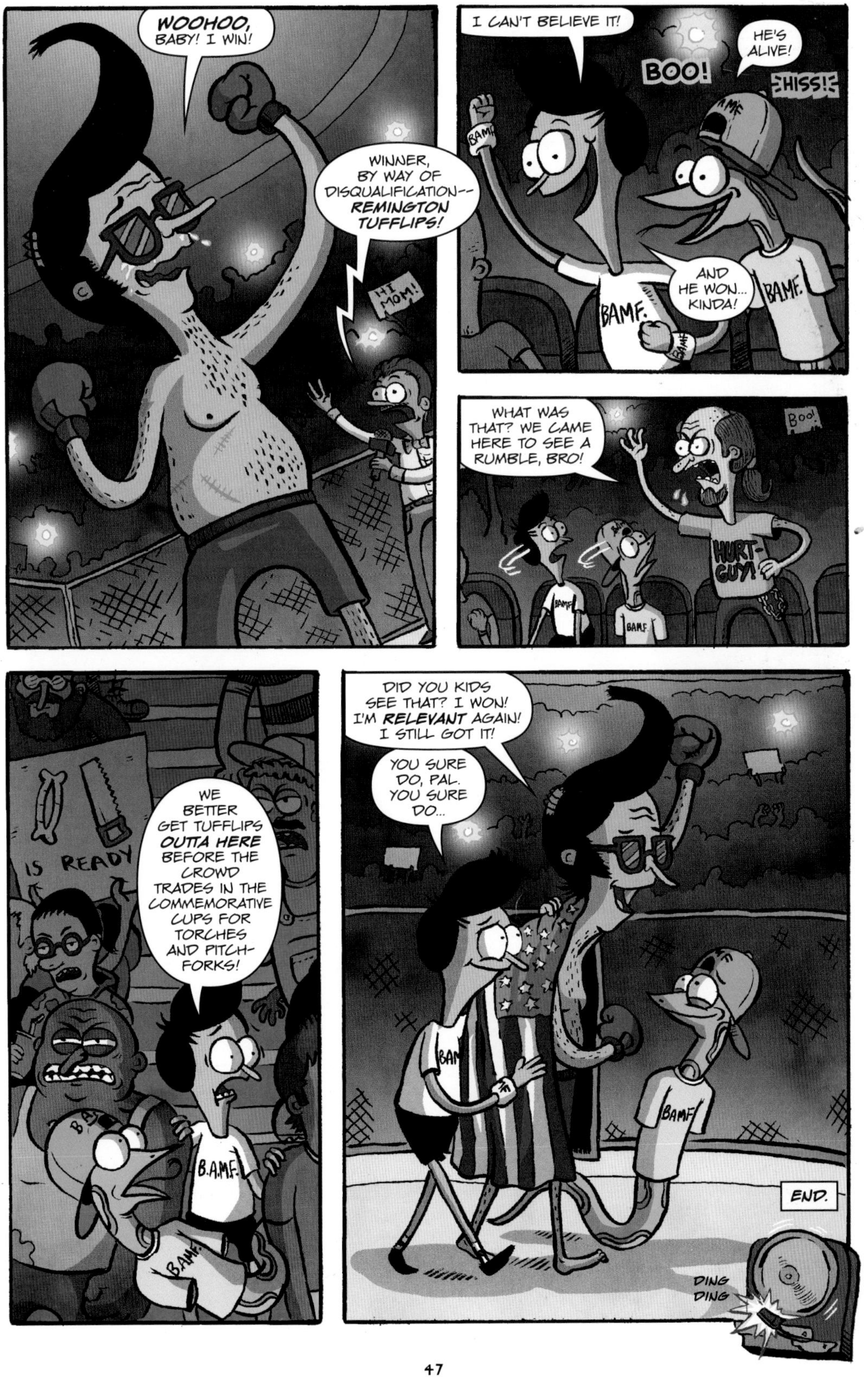
WOOHOO, BABY! I WIN!
WINNER, BY WAY OF DISQUALIFICATION-- REMINGTON TUFFLIPS!
HI MOM!
I CAN'T BELIEVE IT!
BOO!
HE'S ALIVE!
HISS!
AND HE WON... KINDA!
BAMF.
BAMF.
WHAT WAS THAT? WE CAME HERE TO SEE A RUMBLE, BRO!
BOO!
HURT-GUY!
IS READY
WE BETTER GET TUFFLIPS OUTTA HERE BEFORE THE CROWD TRADES IN THE COMMEMORATIVE CUPS FOR TORCHES AND PITCH-FORKS!
B.A.M.F.
DID YOU KIDS SEE THAT? I WON! I'M RELEVANT AGAIN! I STILL GOT IT!
YOU SURE DO, PAL. YOU SURE DO...
END.
DING DING

WATCH OUT FOR PAPERCUTZ

Welcome to the somewhat silly and satirical second SANJAY AND CRAIG graphic novel from Papercutz—those demented dudes dedicated to publishing great graphic novels for all ages. I'm Jim Salicrup, Editor-in-Chief and big-time Andy ("In the future, everyone will beat me up for 15 minutes.") Warhead fan, and I'm here just to let you know what else is going on both at Nickelodeon and Papercutz.

But before we do that, I just wanted to shout out how thrilled I am to be working with Joan Hilty and Bethany Bryan on all our Nickelodeon comics. Joan of course is the comic editor at Nickelodeon, and a veteran comics editor in her own right. I've always respected her work from afar, and now I get to see up close why so many comics writers and artists hold her in such high regard. Joan deals directly with the creators of the various TV series we're doing comics on, and is able to help us create comics that we love, the animators love, and we hope that you love. Bethany works on the Papercutz side of things, and is in constant contact with all of our writers, artists, colorists, and letterers—mostly the awesome Laurie E. Smith and the award-winning Tom Orzechowski, as far as the coloring and lettering is concerned. She's also a great editor, with a children's publishing background, who's able to keep our creators doing what they love while keeping it all on schedule, while editing a gazillion other Papercutz titles as well. (Of course Eric Esquivel, Sam Spina, James Kaminski, Kelsey Wroten, and Steven Wells actually wrote and drew all the stories in this graphic novel and deserve a little credit too...!)

Speaking of which... Have you checked out the premiere BREADWINNERS graphic novel? Just like our SANJAY AND CRAIG graphic novels, it features all-new stories that you've never seen on TV. Here's a quick peek:

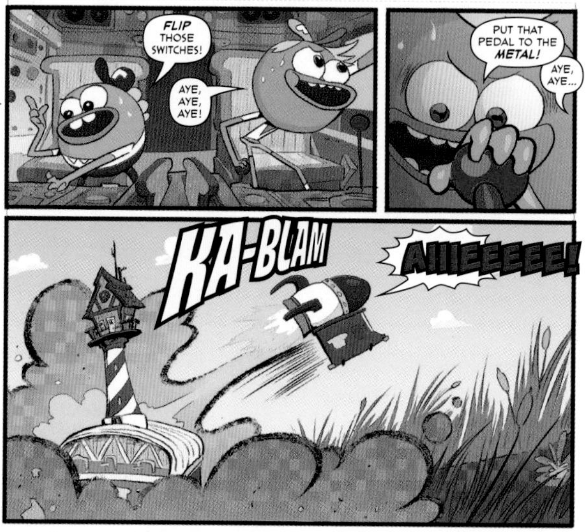
FLIP THOSE SWITCHES!
AYE, AYE, AYE!
PUT THAT PEDAL TO THE METAL!
AYE, AYE...
KA-BLAM
AIIIEEEEE!

And if that wasn't exciting enough, wait till you see the HARVEY BEAKS graphic novel! Here's a peek at that:

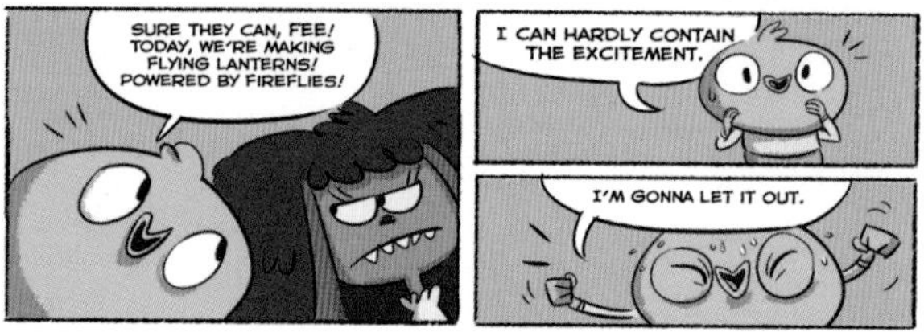
SURE THEY CAN, FEE! TODAY, WE'RE MAKING FLYING LANTERNS! POWERED BY FIREFLIES!
I CAN HARDLY CONTAIN THE EXCITEMENT.
I'M GONNA LET IT OUT.

Now that I'm almost out of room, I still have to mention that there's also a PIG GOAT BANANA CRICKET graphic novel coming too! That's these guys:

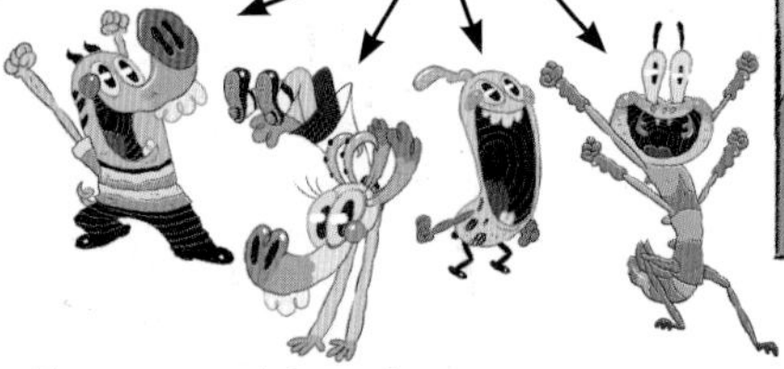

For even more information on these graphic novels (and more) and how to subscribe to NICKELODEON MAGAZINE, be sure to go to Papercutz.com. And be sure to visit www.nickelodeon.tv for latest news, updates, games and more on all your favorite Nickelodeon characters!

Thanks,

Jim

STAY IN TOUCH!

EMAIL:	salicrup@papercutz.com
WEB:	papercutz.com
TWITTER:	@papercutzgn
FACEBOOK:	PAPERCUTZGRAPHICNOVELS
FANMAIL:	Papercutz, 160 Broadway, Suite 700, East Wing, New York, NY 10038

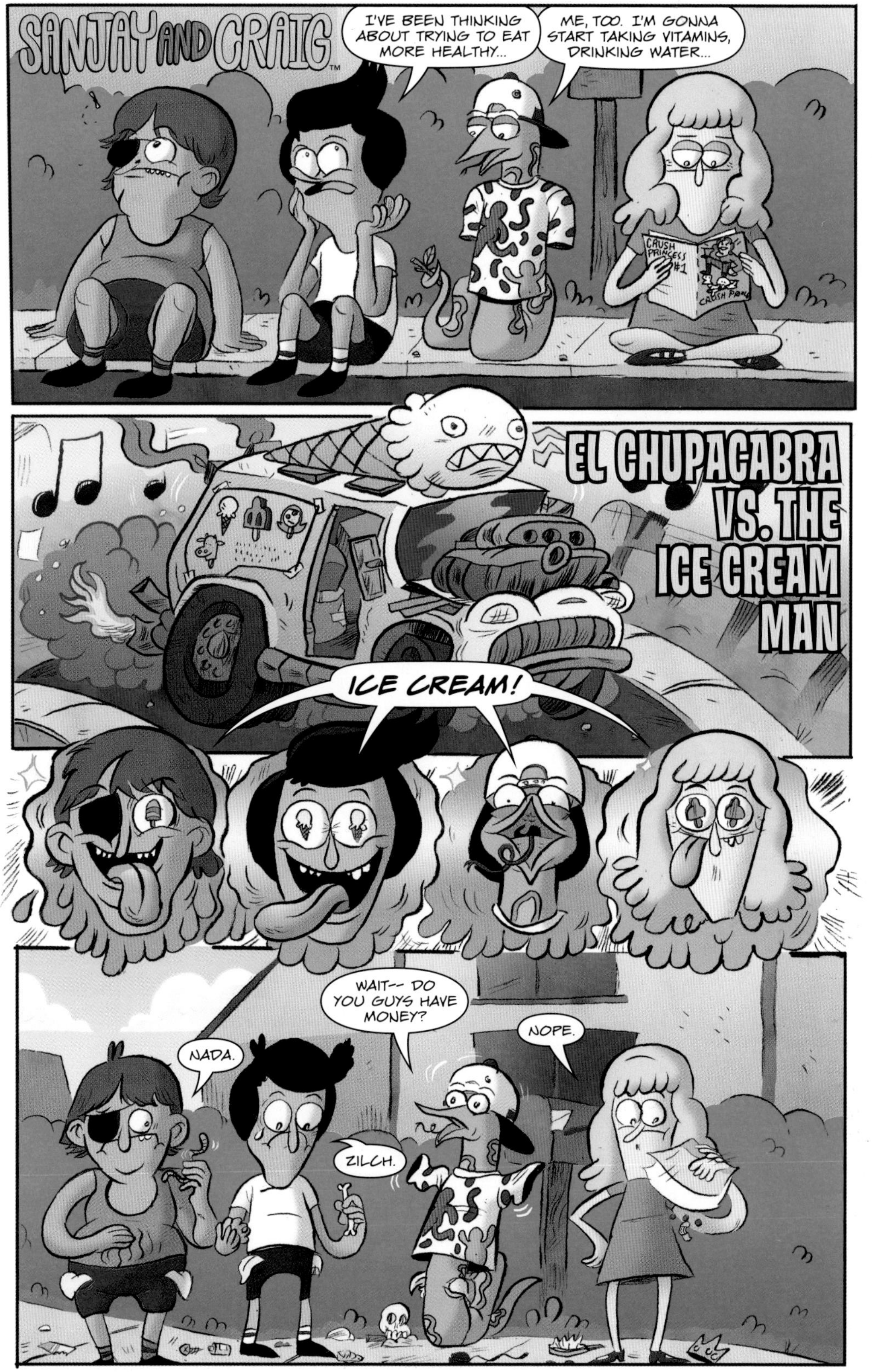
SANJAY AND CRAIG
TM
I'VE BEEN THINKING ABOUT TRYING TO EAT MORE HEALTHY...
ME, TOO. I'M GONNA START TAKING VITAMINS, DRINKING WATER...
CRUSH PRINCESS #1
EL CHUPACABRA VS. THE ICE CREAM MAN
ICE CREAM!
WAIT-- DO YOU GUYS HAVE MONEY?
NADA.
NOPE.
ZILCH.

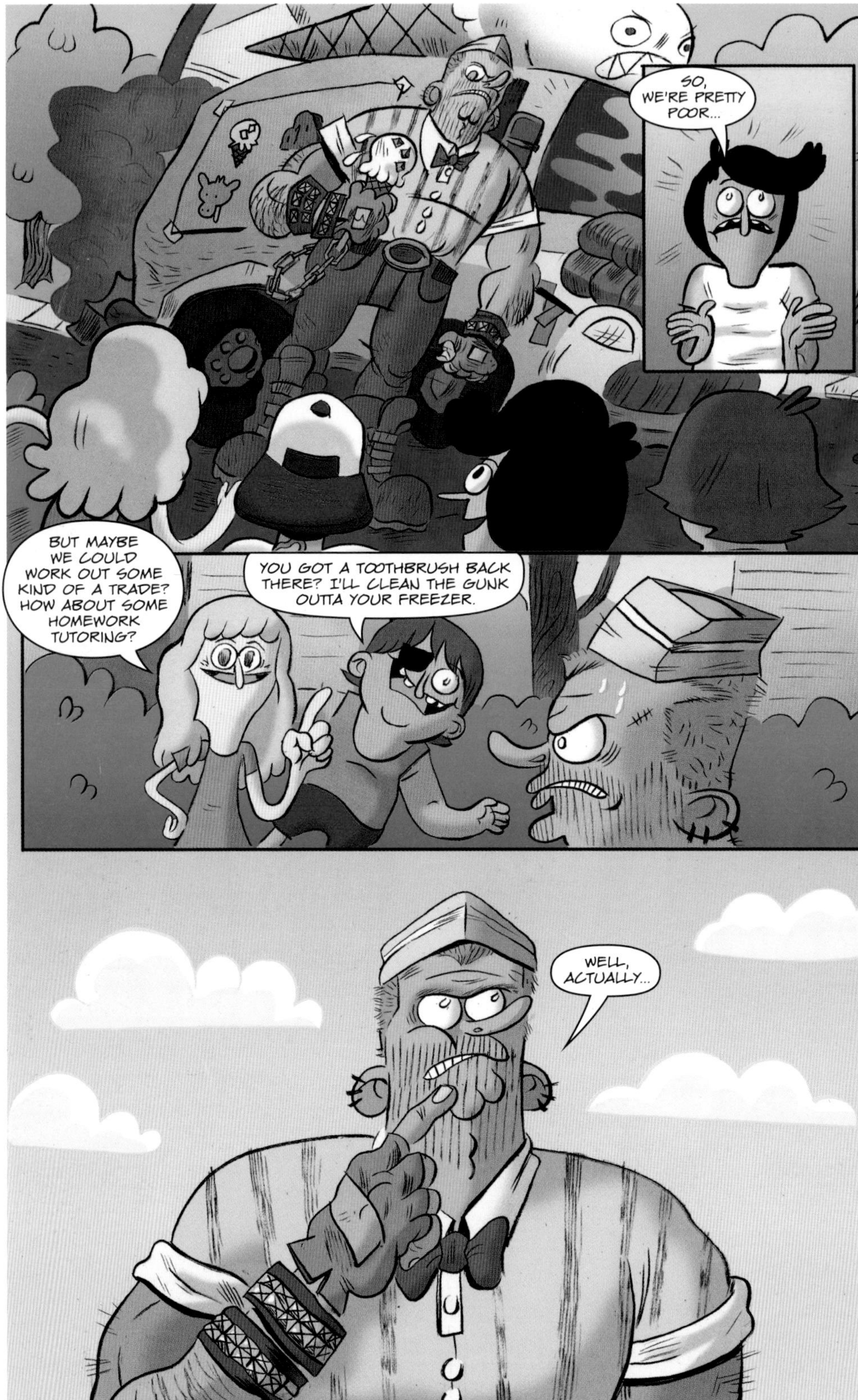
SO, WE'RE PRETTY POOR...
BUT MAYBE WE COULD WORK OUT SOME KIND OF A TRADE? HOW ABOUT SOME HOMEWORK TUTORING?
YOU GOT A TOOTHBRUSH BACK THERE? I'LL CLEAN THE GUNK OUTTA YOUR FREEZER.
WELL, ACTUALLY...

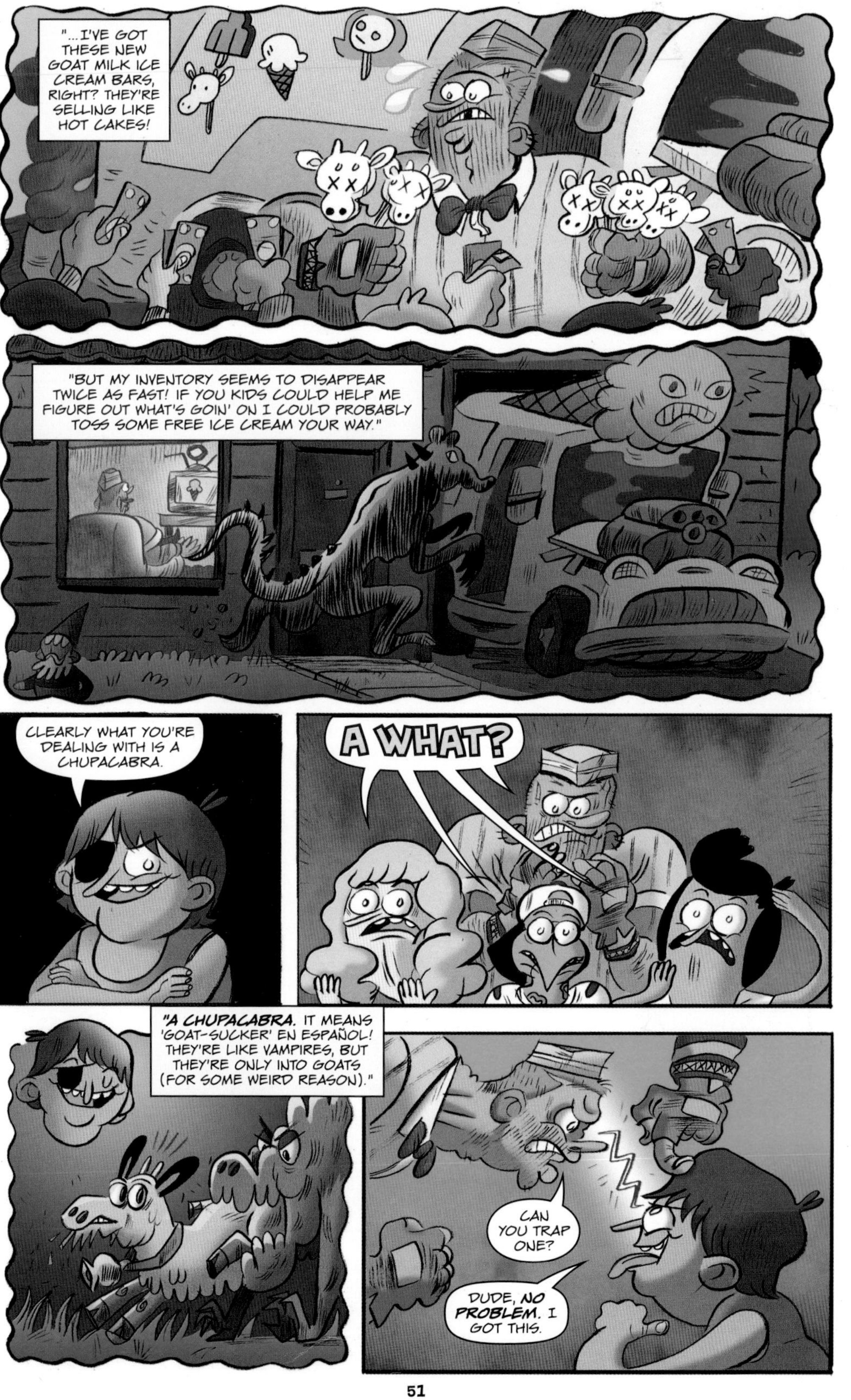
"...I'VE GOT THESE NEW GOAT MILK ICE CREAM BARS, RIGHT? THEY'RE SELLING LIKE HOT CAKES!
"BUT MY INVENTORY SEEMS TO DISAPPEAR TWICE AS FAST! IF YOU KIDS COULD HELP ME FIGURE OUT WHAT'S GOIN' ON I COULD PROBABLY TOSS SOME FREE ICE CREAM YOUR WAY."
CLEARLY WHAT YOU'RE DEALING WITH IS A CHUPACABRA.
A WHAT?
"A CHUPACABRA. IT MEANS 'GOAT-SUCKER' EN ESPAÑOL! THEY'RE LIKE VAMPIRES, BUT THEY'RE ONLY INTO GOATS (FOR SOME WEIRD REASON)."
CAN YOU TRAP ONE?
DUDE, NO PROBLEM. I GOT THIS.

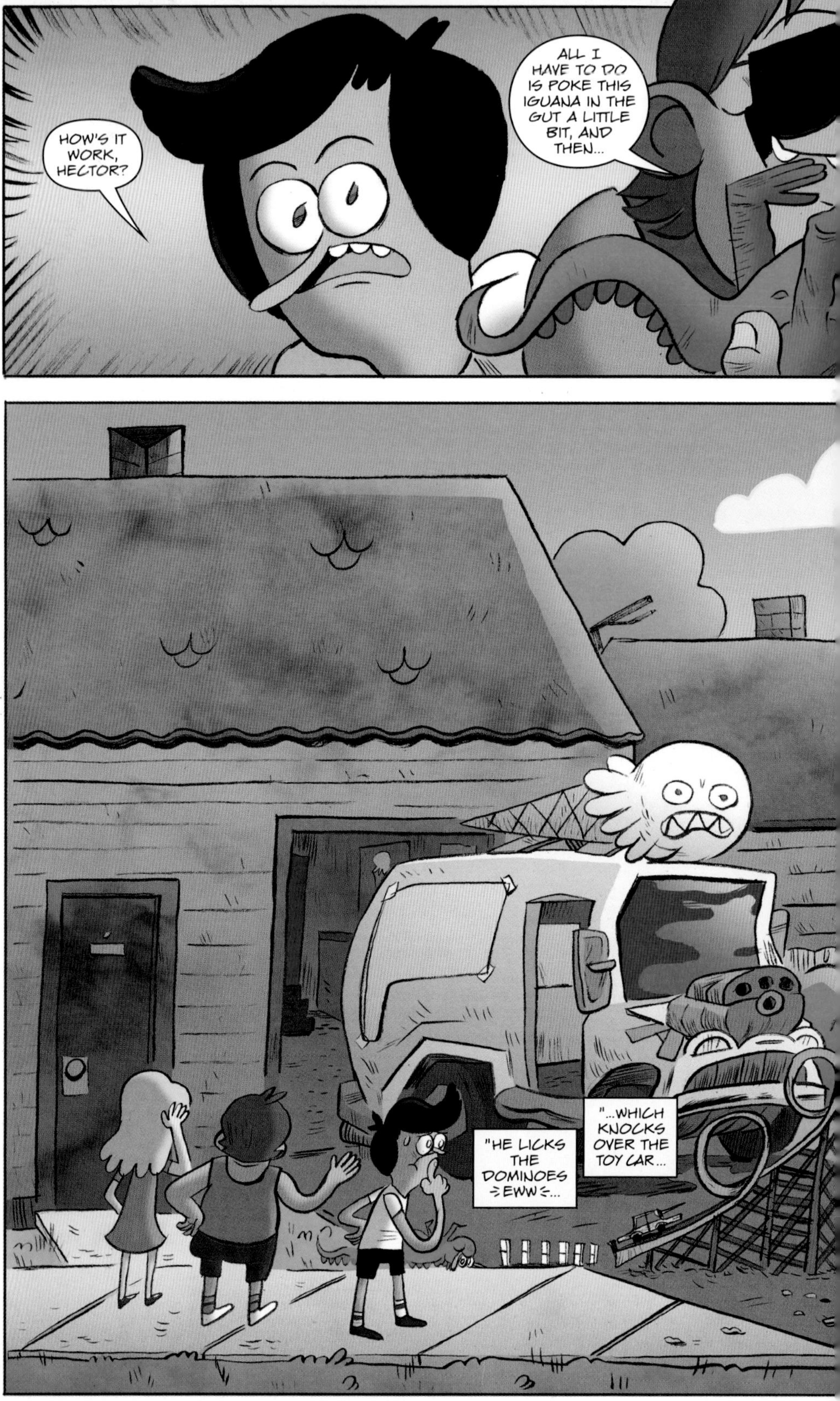
HOW'S IT WORK, HECTOR?
ALL I HAVE TO DO IS POKE THIS IGUANA IN THE GUT A LITTLE BIT, AND THEN...
"HE LICKS THE DOMINOES ≥EWW≤...
"...WHICH KNOCKS OVER THE TOY CAR...

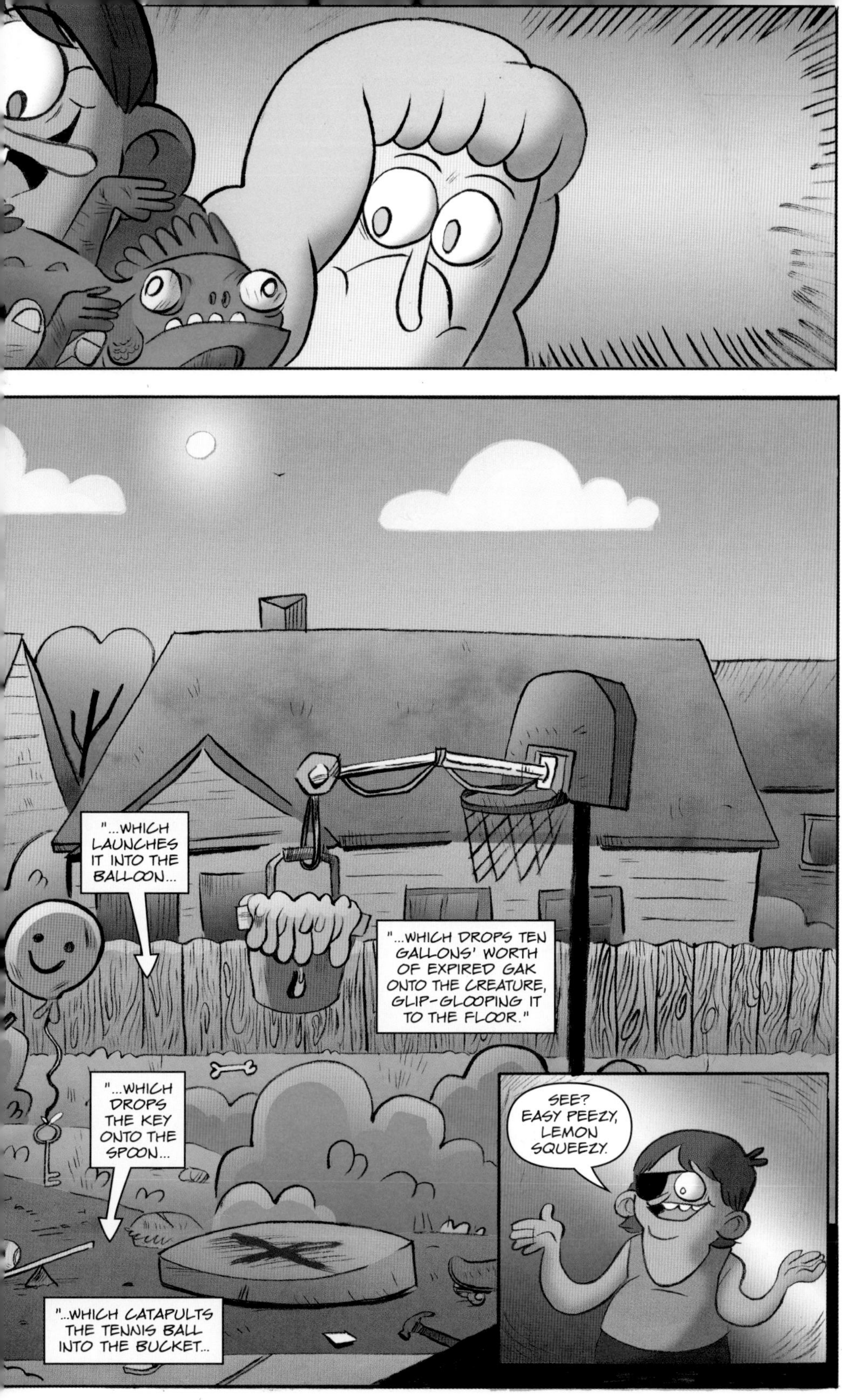
"...WHICH LAUNCHES IT INTO THE BALLOON...
"...WHICH DROPS TEN GALLONS' WORTH OF EXPIRED GAK ONTO THE CREATURE, GLIP-GLOOPING IT TO THE FLOOR."
"...WHICH DROPS THE KEY ONTO THE SPOON...
"...WHICH CATAPULTS THE TENNIS BALL INTO THE BUCKET...
SEE? EASY PEEZY, LEMON SQUEEZY.

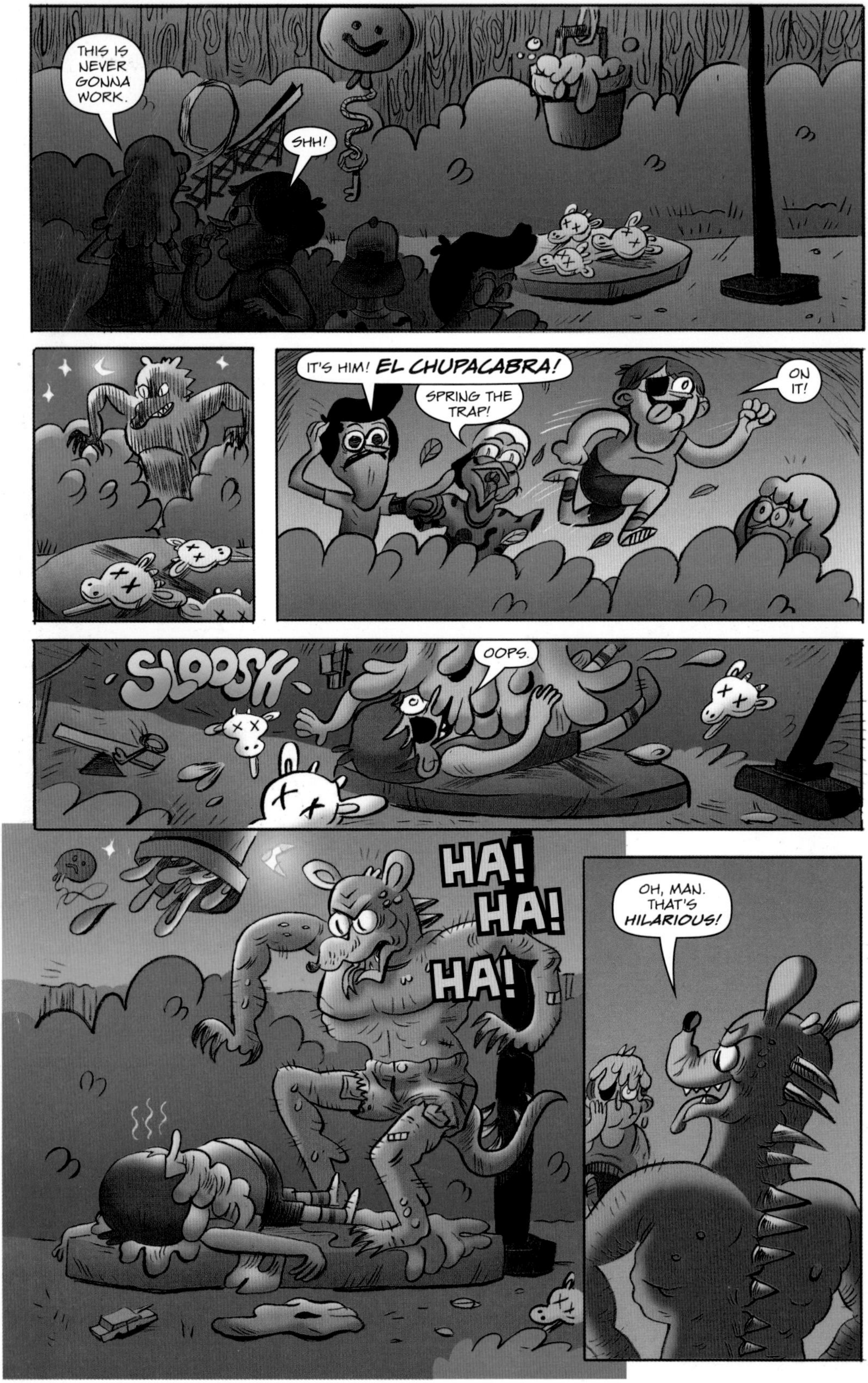

THIS IS NEVER GONNA WORK.
SHH!
IT'S HIM! EL CHUPACABRA!
SPRING THE TRAP!
ON IT!
SLOOSH
OOPS.
HA! HA! HA!
OH, MAN. THAT'S HILARIOUS!

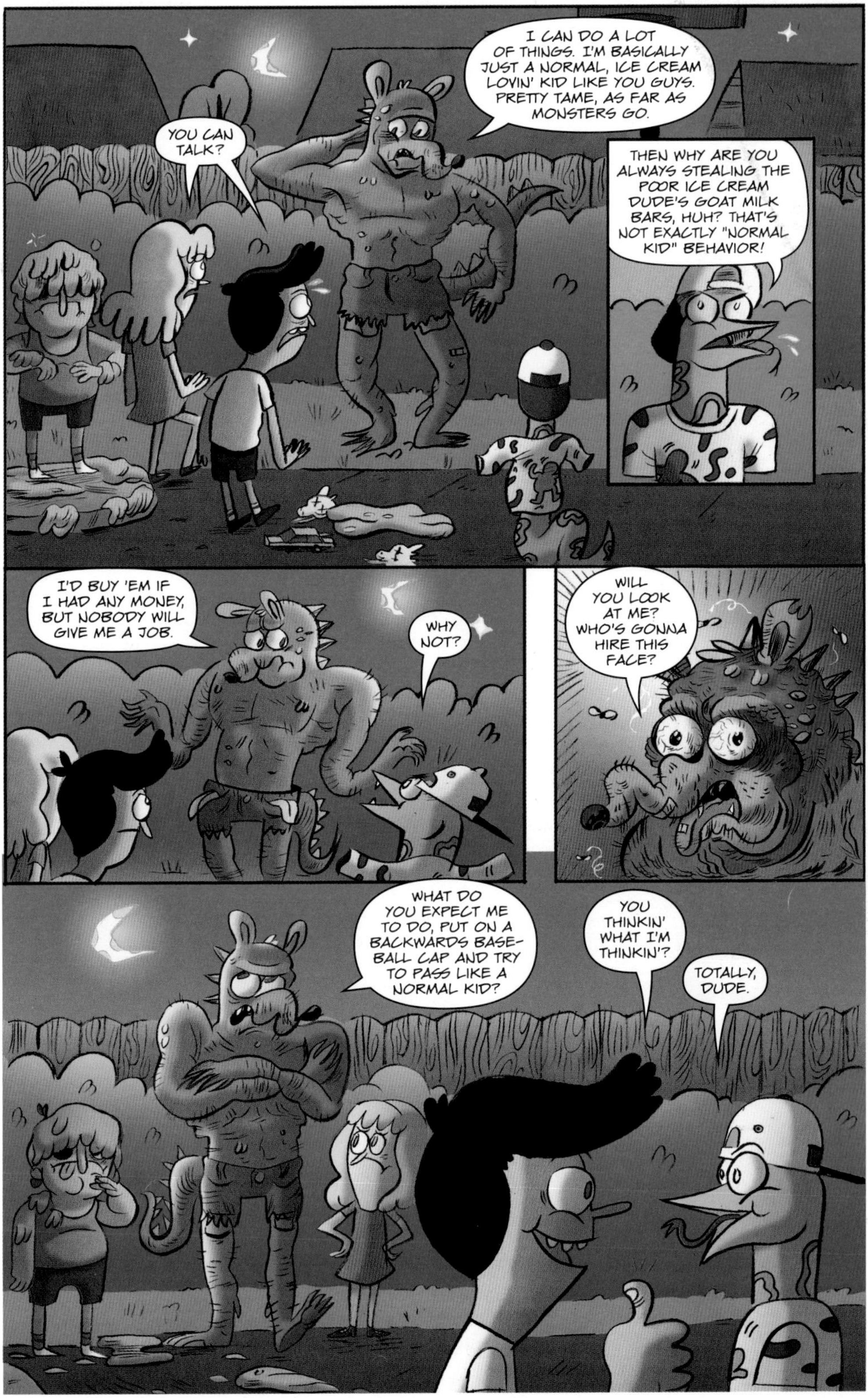
YOU CAN TALK?
I CAN DO A LOT OF THINGS. I'M BASICALLY JUST A NORMAL, ICE CREAM LOVIN' KID LIKE YOU GUYS. PRETTY TAME, AS FAR AS MONSTERS GO.
THEN WHY ARE YOU ALWAYS STEALING THE POOR ICE CREAM DUDE'S GOAT MILK BARS, HUH? THAT'S NOT EXACTLY "NORMAL KID" BEHAVIOR!
I'D BUY 'EM IF I HAD ANY MONEY, BUT NOBODY WILL GIVE ME A JOB.
WHY NOT?
WILL YOU LOOK AT ME? WHO'S GONNA HIRE THIS FACE?
WHAT DO YOU EXPECT ME TO DO, PUT ON A BACKWARDS BASE-BALL CAP AND TRY TO PASS LIKE A NORMAL KID?
YOU THINKIN' WHAT I'M THINKIN'?
TOTALLY, DUDE.

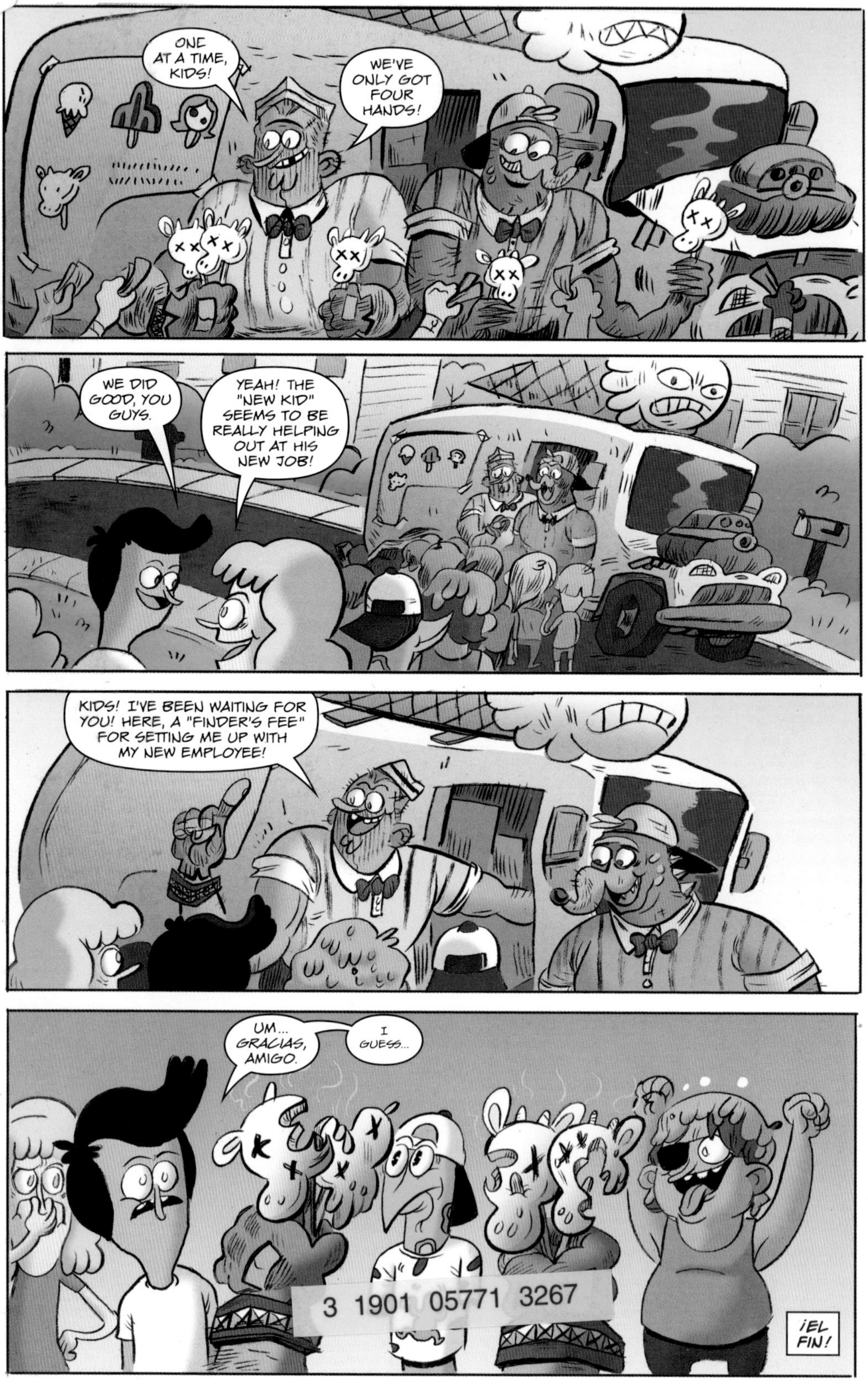
ONE AT A TIME, KIDS!
WE'VE ONLY GOT FOUR HANDS!
WE DID GOOD, YOU GUYS.
YEAH! THE "NEW KID" SEEMS TO BE REALLY HELPING OUT AT HIS NEW JOB!
KIDS! I'VE BEEN WAITING FOR YOU! HERE, A "FINDER'S FEE" FOR SETTING ME UP WITH MY NEW EMPLOYEE!
UM... GRACIAS, AMIGO.
I GUESS...
¡EL FIN!